T0354700

THE RIGHT THING

Also by this author

To So Few

THE RIGHT THING

LEE GRIFFITH

THE RIGHT THING

iUniverse books may be ordered through booksellers or by contacting:

iUniverse
1663 Liberty Drive
Bloomington, IN 47403
www.iuniverse.com
844-349-9409

ISBN: 978-1-6632-5632-4 (sc)
ISBN: 978-1-6632-5637-9 (e)

Library of Congress Control Number: 2023917716

Print information available on the last page.

iUniverse rev. date: 10/05/2023

Dedication

To my wife, Elizabeth Stolberg Griffith.

Contents

Chapter 1..1

Chapter 2..9

Chapter 3...25

Chapter 4...51

Chapter 5...67

Chapter 6...75

Chapter 7...99

Chapter 8..119

Chapter 9..147

Chapter 10...153

Chapter 11...161

Chapter 12...175

Chapter 1

He woke up in a strange room. Why was he here, flat on his back? He looked around. There was an IV stuck into his upper forearm. He had sticky probes all over his chest like he was getting an EKG. There was a strap around his waist so he wouldn't roll off the bed. The clothes around his neck and on his chest looked like a hospital gown. There was a plastic bracelet on his left wrist with his name and rank. Sergeant Ronald Gates, USA. If it had said USN, USAF, or USMC he would mean he was in the Navy, the Air Force, or the Marines. But it said USA, so he was in the Army.

He wasn't sure of much at this point. He was sure he wasn't in the Army, and he was sure his name wasn't Gates.

He closed his eyes. He took a few deep breaths. He had been on an assignment. In Iraq. In Fallujah, or Al-Fallujah as it was known locally. It was about 35 miles west of Baghdad, close to the geographic center of Iraq. How could he remember all that and not remember how he got here? He had been working with a partner. They were supposed to find and take out a sniper. "Looks more like the sniper took me out instead," he said to himself.

Well, enough of this nonsense, he thought. He began to pull the leads that led to all the sensors on his chest, which set off lights and alarm bells like crazy at the hospital nurse station.

He didn't know it, but at that moment, the guy who shot him, the sniper, was running for his life.

Baghdad, Iraq

The sniper was running for the eastern border, trying to escape from Iraq. The cops were after him. He was trying to cross the border into Iran, at night, and escape detection. When it came to escaping detection, he was doing a lousy job of it.

Whap! A bullet hit his hat. There goes my hat! He turned ninety degrees and ran. Whap! A bullet hit his backpack.

"I HATE IT WHEN THEY SHOOT AT ME! I especially HATE IT WHEN THEY HIT ME!"

After sprinting for what seemed forever, he was panting like a dog. His lungs burned. His legs felt like they weighed a ton.

He jumped into a ditch and ran along it, keeping his head low, praying that the terrain would cover him. This escape was going to be a close thing. A very close thing! All he wanted now was a clean escape. A chance to get away from this war that he hated. He wanted to get back to the farm where he could see the sun rise and set, see the stars appear at night, and see the girl he loved so much.

He had no idea how strange life could get. He had no

idea that in a few months he would meet the guy he shot. In fact, he would be asked to work with him.

Months Later
Hindu Kush Mountains, Afghanistan

The two men did meet, and they began to work together. It was a much later that they began to get along.

By the time that they started to speak to each other like normal people, they had been working together for months. They sat alone at the 13,000-foot level on a cold night, shivering. One of them was from the Middle East and was still learning to speak English. The other was an American, an athlete, a college baseball player, lover of a girl who he thought was too smart for him.

"In the end, everything can be taken from you," the American was saying. "When that happens, the only thing you got left is who you are. You have to be righteous."

"What does that mean?"

"It means you do the right thing."

"Where did you hear that?"

"From my fiancée, and her family."

"You learned that from a woman, and her family?"

"Yeah. Right after I learned that they came from Ireland and their family wanted to kill people like me."

"And you asked her to marry you. You crazy? They never accept you. If one of their family kills one of yours, nobody will ever forget it."

3

"No, they will. They will accept me. We can get along now. But you wouldn't believe how it started out with her family."

"You can't get along with them. Cannot! Blood echoes down from father to son. Never forgotten. This I know."

"Not if you are righteous."

"Her family is Irish?"

"Was. On her mother's side. Irish as Paddy's Pig."

"Paddy? Who is Paddy?"

"Forget it."

"You aren't Irish? What is your family?"

"We were from England."

"What did they say when they heard you aren't Irish?"

"They showed me a letter from their cousin who still lives in the old country, in Ireland."

"What did it say?"

"It said they wanted to hang the Protestants and burn all their churches. It also said send money!"

"So, the Irish and the English fight?"

"It's mostly over now, but for years the IRA, that's the Irish Republican Army, tried to kill or blow up everything they could. They wanted Northern Ireland to be part of Ireland instead of part of the United Kingdom along with England, Scotland, and Wales."

"And her family wanted to hang you and now you want to marry her? You CRAZY!"

"No, we want to bury the hatchet."

"Bury the hatchet? Hatchet?"

"Yeah. Like an axe. Bury it. Put the guns away. Make peace. However, you would say it."

"Where I came from, blood is never forgotten."

"That is why there won't be peace in the Middle East. But there could be."

The man from the Middle East could hardly believe how he got here. The relationship between these two was tenuous, for good reason. At an earlier time, they were enemies, and the man from the Middle East was a sniper and had put a bullet in him. Now they were friends. Sort of.

They thought they were operating undetected at the 13,000-foot level in Afghanistan. A well-aimed shot dispelled that notion. It was only dumb luck that had saved him. He slipped, and the shot cleared his head and hit the boulder behind him. The next shot sprayed shards of granite in his face.

The Taliban had somehow found them and nearly surrounded them. To stay alive, they had to get out of there, and fast. They traversed to their left for four hundred meters on a ledge that started out six inches wide and gradually vanished.

Abdul had spent years in the mountains, but what they did now was dangerous beyond description.

"I think this is the most dangerous thing I have ever done!" Abdul shouted.

"Don't think. Just do."

"You are an idiot. What do we do now?"

"Get above them. They won't expect it."

"They won't expect it because it cannot be done."

"See this crack? Right here, on this granite face."

"We climb up this crack, and higher up there is a chimney we can use."

He was a Sergeant in the Marine Corps. Everyone called him Stinko.

He jammed his fingers into the crack and jammed his toes sideways. He began to move up the rock face. After a while, the crack got wider and easier to climb. He made it to a small ledge, jammed a chock into the rock, anchored himself in and dropped a rope to his partner. His partner grabbed the rope, rapidly tied a bowline around his waist, and followed him up "What's next?" Abdul queried.

"Stay tied in. Anchor into this chock. I'll traverse a bit and get into the chimney... I think."

"Don't think, idiot! Get moving!"

He made the traverse somehow to the base of the chimney and started to ascend. It got easier a little higher up. He set another chock, anchored into it, and yelled back to his partner. "Work your way over. Get below me. Then come up this chimney."

When both were in the chimney, he started ascending again. Few people could do this as rapidly as he could. Every hundred feet or so he anchored in and helped his partner catch up. They reached a point where the mountain rounded out a bit and they could scramble up using their feet and hands.

"Slow down you bastard! You are killing me!" Abdul shouted.

"My, my! Haven't we picked up a vocabulary!" Stinko said between gasps for air.

They were clawing their way up this brutal mountain that went up forever.

"We're at 14,000 feet and climbing you idiot! Slow down!"

"Can't slow down," Stinko shouted.

"Slow down!"

"This is your country! You should be at home here!"

"It's not my country! Abdul blurted out." He had rarely admitted it to the Americans.

"If we slow down, they will catch us," Stinko said.

"Won't happen."

"Ping! A bullet bounced off a rock next to Abdul's head."

"See! I told you! Stinko shouted."

More bullets hit the rocks around them.

"That one was close!" Stinko blurted out.

They tumbled together behind a boulder.

"Now what?"

"We get over this ridge and hightail it down the other side."

"Ridge? Ridge?"

"Oh, vocabulary failing you? The top, idiot! We go over the top!"

Stinko took a breath and started going uphill again at the speed of heat. After a few seconds he realized he was alone.

"Abdul! What are you doing?"

"Wait!"

"Wait? Wait? Let's go!"

"Wait!"

Abdul had pulled his Dragunov sniper rifle off his back and verified that his 7.62-millimeter match-grade ammo was ready to use. He took five quick breaths then five slow, deep breaths. He peered around the edge of the boulder and saw what he wanted. The Taliban were coming up the mountain after them, and the lack of cover that had been the curse of this mission was now working against the Taliban.

The sniper carefully moved his camouflaged weapon around the boulder, took a breath in, let it out, waited between heartbeats, and fired. The bullet landed right in the Taliban's forehead.

"That's one," Abdul said.

One brave Taliban fighter did not see his comrade fall, and he kept climbing up the mountain. Abdul fired.

"That's two." Another head shot.

At that point five Taliban started moving up the mountain. Blam! Blam! Two shots in rapid succession. Two shots to the body. They were coming too fast for pinpoint accuracy now.

"Stinko! Stinko! Some help!"

Stinko opened fire from a higher position using his M4 carbine. His first shot hit, but everyone disappeared after that. Then 15 Taliban started shooting at the same time!

"My God! How did we get into this?"

Chapter 2

Abdul packed rapidly. The Baghdad police sought him for murder of one of their own. He was sick of the war in Iraq and would have been happy to leave here under any circumstance, but now escape was imperative.

His eye burned terribly. A bullet from a gunshot had hit the furniture in front of him and drove splinters into his right eye. The Al Qaeda doctor removed the splinters from the eye, placed a patch over it and handed him some pain medicine. Abdul had not taken the medicine yet because he needed all his senses to make his escape.

While in his apartment Abdul grabbed his pack. In the pack he stuffed the head scarf called a kaffiyeh, a wool jacket, a first aid kit, a sweater, a poncho, a pair of gloves, six pairs of socks, and some dried food. As an afterthought he jammed a burqa into the pack. You never know when you will need a disguise. He pulled money from four different stashes he had in the room. The smallest stash of cash had been in the bed mattress, with larger ones in the floor, in the wall and in the ceiling. He wrapped a money belt around his waist, put on a shirt and sweater, and picked up the backpack. The whole evolution took three minutes. He heard a siren from a police car drawing closer. He looked out the window and saw a police car pull up in front of his

9

apartment building. Abdul raced out of the room and ran down the back steps to the back alley.

Abdul's supervisor was the man they called "The Captain," who met him with a car three blocks from his apartment, at the place they had agreed upon. Abdul climbed into the passenger seat. At first the captain did not recognize him. Abdul usually wore a dishdasha (ankle length robe) with traditional headgear. Now he wore a ball cap and a pair of coveralls he had swiped from a construction site. The beard was gone, leaving only a mustache.

Abdul had been fighting against the Russians in Afghanistan, and later against the Northern Alliance. After he had been in Afghanistan five years the Americans came. The Al Qaeda leadership moved him from Afghanistan to Iraq, to fight the Americans. When the local authorities started to cooperate with the Americans, he started to fight against the local authorities as well. Now the Iraqi cops wanted him for murder, for killing cops in Baghdad.

"Where are you going, Abdul?" the Captain asked.

"Do the police have a dragnet out for me?" Abdul responded with his own question.

"I have no idea. You aren't in the papers or on television if that is what you mean. Why the change of appearance?"

"I need to look different. Let's go to the train station. I need you to buy a train ticket for me. They may be looking for me. I'll give you the money."

The Captain came out of the train station carrying a newspaper that he bought there.

He handed the money back to Abdul. "It's no good, Abdul. Your picture is on the billboards on a wanted poster."

"I'll get on the train at a station a couple of stops down the line. Maybe they won't be looking so hard there."

"You can use this car, but I can't drive you. I'll have Omar drive you."

Abdul had second thoughts while they were on the way to pick up Omar. He figured the police only had to send a message to the other towns on the railroad line to notify them that Abdul was wanted and possibly traveling by train. They could be waiting for him at his destination. He pictured the scene: he gets off the train and gets picked up. Great plan, Abdul! If he went south on the train, he would be in Iraq for 300 miles. If he went east by car, he could be out of the country in about 60 miles. The closest border had an appeal to him that he could not resist.

"What about Rahim?" Abdul asked.

"What about him?" The captain replied.

"Rahim is from Bakhtaran, in Iran. He could be useful."

"OK. I'll have Rahim drive you."

The captain pressed a piece of paper into Abdul's hand.

"There is an address there. You can reach me," the Captain said.

"Why are you doing this for me?" Abdul asked.

"You are the best shooter who ever worked for me."

"Helping me could get you in trouble. It could harm the cause."

LEE GRIFFITH

"Let me worry about that, Abdul. Your job is to get out, now."

Abdul said nothing.

The Captain spoke from the heart. "There is no spiritual basis for what we do for Al Qaeda. That's long gone. Abdul, you worked for this cause for six years. You were the best we ever had. I owe it to you."

Abdul extended his hand to shake hands.

The captain embraced him. Abdul realized he was leaving one of the few friends he had in this life.

Abdul and Rahim were driving in an old car that looked like it had seen better days. They no sooner got out of town than they ran into a checkpoint.

That was a brilliant decision, ABDUL YOU IDIOT! He cursed himself for choosing to go by car instead of by train. Rahim was driving and he slowed down and stopped beside the guard. "Now what?" he asked himself.

"Let me see your ID!" The guard demanded. "Where are you going?" The Iraqi security officer was looking at the driver.

"I'm from Bakhtaran, in Iran. I'm going home."
"Why?"
"Since when do you need an excuse to go home?"
"What about him?" The guard pointed to Abdul.
"He's with me."

The guard turned his attention to Abdul. "Why are you leaving?"

"I lost my job when I injured my eye. Now I can't get work."

"How did that happen?"

"What?"

"Your eye."

"I was on a construction job. It was an accident."

"Where?"

"West Baghdad."

"What project?"

"The Nahrain School."

"How did you hurt your eye?"

"One of the workers picked up a board. He had the board over his shoulder. I turned around and walked into it."

The guard believed him. "You can pass," he said.

They drove away from the checkpoint.

"That was a good lie you told to that guard, Rahim said. Why did you say what you did?"

"Because the Nahrain School project is real. He could have checked."

"What would you say if he asked you who the foreman was?"

"I saw the foreman when we were in the city. He was a kid I knew from school."

"Did you work there?"

"No."

"What if the guard asked questions you couldn't answer?"

"What if, what if? Obviously at some point an alibi

breaks down. It is better if it breaks down later rather than sooner."

Abdul had not picked this life; it had picked him. His father beat him from the time he was a child. The last time was when he was 15 and his father was beating him with a wrench. Abdul picked up a brick and slammed it into father's head. His father was dead within minutes. Abdul dumped his father's body into the Euphrates River in the middle of the night. He didn't know what to do. He went to the mosque before the morning prayer to seek the advice of the imam, who sent him to join the mujahadein in Afghanistan. It was the mujahadein who discovered his talent with a rifle. He trained with them for months and became a sniper. He worked as a sniper for six years. When the Americans overwhelmed the Taliban in Afghanistan, Abdul was ordered to go into hiding on a farm in south Afghanistan and ordered to lay low. It was there he met Meena. It was the only time that his life made any sense. He loved to work with her in the field. He loved to watch her while she worked, and he loved learning how to take care of the machinery in her father's barn. Maybe it was the time and the place, maybe it was the soft curve of her body and the way she walked, the sound of her voice, the smell of her hair. Maybe it was life on a farm. It was all of that. He had a feeling for the land. He had a feeling for her. But why did she stop writing? She was a woman born and raised in Afghanistan, but she could both read and write.

Rahim the driver broke Abdul's reverie "Where are you going in Iran?"

"I haven't a clue." Abdul lied. He knew that he wouldn't be staying in Iran.

Rahim said, "I'll give you the address of my parents in Bakhtaran. They can give you some food and supplies. You might need them. I'll give them a note so they will know you can be trusted."

"Thank you."

Abdul appreciated the offer. He would accept the note that Rahim gave him, but he would not use it. A known destination made him predictable, and for seven years he had stayed alive by being anything but predictable.

Abdul's plan was to get to the farm in Afghanistan. To do that, he would go to Arak in Iran then go by train for about 600 miles southeast to Kerman, Iran. From there he had another 350 miles or so across the desert to the border of Afghanistan. The less people knew his plan, the better.

Abdul and Rahim drove in the car the Captain provided. They drove through town and up to the border that went into Iran. There was a line of cars a hundred yards long and border guards were inspecting the cars inside and out.

"How many times have you crossed here?" Abdul asked.

"Four or five, why?" Rahim replied.

"Do they do inspections like this every time?"

"No, this is the first time there is an inspection."

"Get out of line, let's go."

"What?"

15

"Just do it!"

Rahim the driver pulled the car out of the line and heard a border guard shout at him.

"You! Halt! Halt!"

"Go!" Abdul implored.

"But he's got a gun! He's raising it!"

"Go! Go! Get going!"

The guard raised the rifle and fired. Rahim looked in the rear-view mirror and saw the flame appear at the muzzle and a bullet smashed through the rear window.

"Step on it!" Abdul shouted!

They roared out of the border area and back toward the center of town. Once out of sight of the border guards Rahim slowed down and headed south.

"That was close!" Then Rahim shouted. "THAT WAS REALLY CLOSE!"

"It's always close." Abdul replied.

"What? You mean you've been in a situation like this before?"

"You mean shot at? Yes, like too many times to count for the last six years."

"I've never been in it this close. Where did the bullet go? Can you see an exit point?"

Abdul looked around and could find none.

"Must have been a magic bullet," Abdul replied. "It disappeared."

He had a moment to collect his thoughts. Here he was, with no sight in his right eye, which was patched. He was in pain. He was sought by the cops. He was in a car that belonged to one of his few friends. Now the car was probably known by the police. What a mess.

Abdul reached into his pocket and pulled out the equivalent of $100 in Iraq's currency, the dinar.

"Here." Abdul said. "Take this for the Captain to repair the window."

"That's good of you, man, but the Captain has enough money."

"Go ahead, take it. I owe him."

"That may be true, but I stole this car a week ago. In about another hour I'll steal another one and leave this car where it can't be found."

"You can do that?"

"That is what I do." Rahim replied. "That's why I'm on the team. I hotwire cars. Cars, trucks, taxis, I hotwire them all. I should be a legend."

They ran into an ambush. Abdul jumped out of the car and ran. A bullet knocked his hat off, then another bullet hit his backpack. He got into a ditch and stayed low and out of sight for a long way. He realized that the cops would search for him in the ditch, so he climbed out and found a low spot of terrain and lay down in it. If he didn't move, they wouldn't see him. He stayed there, in the low spot on the edge of the desert and waited until the moon set. By then it was very dark.

After dark Abdul crossed the border from Iraq to Iran, about five miles south of the town. He had acquired Iraqi,

Iranian, and Afghani currency during the past year. After crossing the border, he hiked back to the city that was on the Iranian side of the border. There he bought a case of fruit which he traded with a truck driver for a ride to Arak. Abdul rode up in the passenger seat with the driver.

"Why do you want to go to Arak?" The driver asked.

"I'm going to help out my brother with his store." Abdul lied.

It was a good story, Abdul thought. It would have been true too, if he had a brother, and his brother had a store.

The driver kept asking him questions. Abdul tried to avoid the questions by pretending to go to sleep.

The driver dropped Abdul off by a fruit stand. Abdul bought some fruit and waited until the truck was out of sight. He then walked via a roundabout route to the train station where he bought a train ticket. While Abdul was purchasing the train ticket the driver, who had given him a ride in the truck, drove to the local police station and asked to be paid for information that he was willing to give them. After less than a minute the driver realized he would not be paid, so he simply told the police that he had given a ride to a man and dropped him off near the Arak train station. The man had a patch over one eye, he seemed nervous, and appeared to want to avoid questions. The police were having a busy night, so they did nothing with the information for several hours, until the activity slowed down. Then the police dispatcher received an APB saying a suspected police killer from Iraq was in the area, wearing a patch over one eye. The police dispatcher remembered he had heard about a guy with an eye patch. After a discussion with the watch captain the dispatcher was directed to pass the information to the transportation points in town.

Once the train was well out of town, Abdul felt the tightness begin to leave him. He slept. He awakened and started thinking of Meena and her supple body. He remembered their first kiss, in the barn on the farm. He remembered pulling her to him. He slept again.

Abdul rode the train as far as Kerman. For the last few stops he noticed there were police on the platform who were stopping and questioning the men who got off the train.

Abdul went into the toilet compartment on the train, removed his shirt and sweater, rolled up his pant legs, and slipped into the burqa. His eyes were visible, but the rest of his body was covered. The shoes could get me in trouble, and I sure hope they don't notice this mustache! He could hold the burqa in front of his face. He pulled a razor out of the backpack and shaved carefully. He didn't leave the toilet until the train stopped.

He got off the train at Kerman and walked up the street using short strides because he wore a woman's clothing. He entered a dark alley and got out of the burqa. He pulled the shirt and sweater out of the backpack and put them on. He rolled down his pant legs. He walked out of the back of the alley and entered a small café where he could get a meal. Several locals ate there. Some smoked a hookah filled with tobacco.

After the meal and several cups of sweet tea he walked out of the café into the night. The temperature was mild for winter. He had enough cash for a hotel room, but he preferred to sleep outside, save his money, and avoid a place where he had to use ID. He walked up the street and noticed that the boys who had been in the café were now following him. He turned the corner at the end of the block and walked right into the rest of their gang.

"Where you going?" The gang member in front of him asked.

That was the last thing Abdul could remember. He regained consciousness on the sidewalk, with his cheek on the concrete and his head aching. He sat up against a building and breathed slowly. He still had the patch over his right eye and his head ached from being hit in the head with a pipe. He rubbed his hand across his waist. His money belt was gone.

Where to go? If he went to a construction site, he wouldn't be seen until morning. A warehouse might have a guard or a camera system. He walked up the street. There were a few shops that were all locked with the type of garage door that rolls down to keep intruders out and to protect the glass in the store front. Every now and then there was a food store. He found an alley behind a food store with a dumpster that he crawled behind. He took the first of the pain killers the doctor had given him. He lay down and slept.

He awoke during the night, drank some water, and slept some more. He awakened several times before daylight. He felt the pouch he had sewn into the inside of his pant leg at the thigh. That was his stash for Iranian money, which felt like it was still intact. He had another stash on each shoulder blade, also concealed, which held his Afghani money. It felt like these stashes were also intact. Abdul had never heard of Murphy's law, but Abdul believed that things go wrong all the time, and you had better have a plan B. When plan B fails, it's good to have plan C. That is why he had so many spare stashes for money.

At first light he retrieved some of the Iranian money and made his way to a café. He had a light meal. When the merchants started selling their wares, he bought several bottles of water and made his way to the main highway that led out into the desert. It took him two days to get across the Iranian desert. Near the border he was able to trade his Iranian money for Afghani currency. It took another two days to make it to Kandahar in Afghanistan. This was down toward the southern part of Afghanistan, where there were mountains to the north and flatter terrain to the south. Meena's farm was not far from there. Would he be welcome there?

His head still hurt, but not as bad as it did before. The eye patch had to go. He did not want anything that would identify him as the fugitive from Baghdad. Abdul spent almost a week in Kandahar, regaining his strength, tanning his face where the patch had been and letting his eyesight slowly improve. He moved to a different part of the city each night. After the week he caught rides to the region where Meena lived. He had to walk the last few miles to their farm.

As he walked up the road to the farmhouse Abdul could see a truck approaching him, driven by Meena's father, Wasim, who had one hand on the steering wheel and one hand on a shotgun.

Abdul wondered what kind of reception he would get.

"Abdul, you are back?"

"It's me. Are you going to use that shotgun on me?"

"Don't give me any excuses!" Wasim smiled. He always liked Abdul.

Wasim explained more. "No, Abdul, unfortunately we have had nothing but trouble since you left."

"What happened?"

"Remember the time you shot the poachers who tried to steal our harvest of poppies? The next time we had a harvest, and everything was loaded on the trucks for shipment to market when a new group of Taliban came, only this time you were not there to help us. The poachers were armed with rifles, and they took everything. I got nothing for a whole season of work. Nothing! If that happens to us again, we will have to sell the farm."

"I'll help you." Abdul volunteered.

"Why should you?"

Abdul did not answer directly.

"I'll help you no matter what." He realized there may be shooting again.

"Is the family OK?" Abdul asked.

"Yes, but I don't think you will like it. Meena is engaged to be married."

"Engaged?" He couldn't breathe. He felt like someone had punched him in the stomach. His face turned pale. He felt sick.

"When?"

"Why don't you ask her? She can tell you. It is almost time for supper. Get in the truck, you can join us."

Abdul followed Wasim through the front door. When Meena saw him, she gasped.

"What … are you doing here?" she asked.

"I thought you might need someone to pull rocks out of the field."

"City boy, you get tired too fast! You are not much of a field hand."

"Then I'll watch you do it," he replied.

Nobody spoke. The mother and father watched, but Abdul and Meena just stared at each other.

They had a good meal. They talked for a while after dinner. Finally, Wasim showed Abdul a couch where he could sleep. He laid down that night and listened as the winter rain beat on the rooftop.

"You have great luck with everything, you fool," he told himself. The girl you love is engaged to somebody else, the farm you dreamed of working on is going broke, and you volunteered your services for something that could become a shooting war.

Chapter 3

Zak started his shift at the 28th Combat Support Hospital in the Green Zone in Iraq with a giant hangover. Two godforsaken tours in this godforsaken place! Two tours with two months to go on this tour and two guys who should be working the shift are out sick, not working because they got the shits. The two guys who actually are working this shift are spending half their time on the toilet. The whole place has the flu. This day was going badly. This shift was going badly. It started from the moment he walked in the door. First, they brought in the Black Hawk helicopters with wounded from an IED explosion. Right after that they brought in the Americans from the helo. Then the wounded who were not Americans came in in droves. This time they had Iraqi women and children who were badly wounded. The small staff handled the workload, but it took hours. Then he learned that his relief was down with the flu and most of the next shift couldn't make it either. He would have to pull 24 hours straight on the job. When it rains, it pours.

In the eighteenth hour of his shift a Black Hawk brought in a couple of American wounded, both shot up badly. One was in Army camouflage, the other was a Marine. The two were brought into the ICU at the same time. This is when his career as a medic in the Army took a decided turn for the worse. The first wounded man had taken automatic rifle fire across his chest, shredding his shirt, and ripping up his pectorals and abdomen. The second guy had one nasty neck wound that caused bleeding that may be fatal. The blood on their uniforms had begun to dry out and smell. Holy ... this guy stinks! The doctor blurted out. "Get them out of these filthy uniforms!" Of all the stinky soldiers in a stinky war, these guys smell the worst!

Working with another medic, Zak got the two out of the blood-soaked uniforms and into hospital garb. It was about then that a mortar shell rocked the place and the lights blinked out for a moment. There were electric monitors on both wounded men, but they did not seem to be working. Zak noticed that the guy's dog tags were on the floor. He picked them up and read them. Ronald Gates. He started to put the dog tags around the guy's neck but then he saw the bandages on the guy's neck wounds. Hey, this other guy was Ronald something or other. Then the second mortar rocked the floor. Zak bumped the gurney and somehow the IV bag disconnected. Ronald Stepovich, that was the other guy's name. Zak reconnected the IV and turned to administer to the guy with the chest wound. This one didn't look too good. Zak got the head surgeon to check him out, but it was too late. He had no pulse and all attempts to revive him failed.

The other guy (Ronald Gates, they thought) appeared to be going downhill fast. Then he too lost his heartbeat and was declared dead.

Two Ronalds came in together. Two Ronalds died here together. Figure the odds. What a rotten shift.

The bossy young doctor came around shortly thereafter and stuck her stethoscope on one corpse, then the other. "Hey! This one has a pulse!"

Couldn't be, Zak thought. The head surgeon had just pronounced him dead, and the head surgeon is god. They had unplugged the guy just a moment before.

"Get this guy back on the IV now! Jesus, what do you people call medicine around here?"

Zak hated this new doctor. She was short. She had short hair. She had short patience. She had a short temper. And she was always right. That's what irked him more than anything. When HE was wrong, SHE was right, and she was always there to prove it. She was so annoying!

"He feels cold. Get a warm blanket. What's this guy's name? Here's a dog tag. Gates! Ronald Gates. Let's get a chart going on this guy. Come on people!" she demanded.

Two Weeks Later

"My name is not Gates!" Ronnie mumbled.

"Take it easy soldier. You have had a hard time. You've been in a coma for two weeks."

"I am not a soldier. I am a Marine. And my name is NOT GATES!" he shouted.

"Mind your manners soldier. You may be in a hospital, but this is a military unit."

"So, you are a Marine, are you? What is your unit?"

Ronnie drew a blank. He remembered the Corps. He remembered his friends in the unit. He remembered Fallujah. He could not remember the name and number of his unit.

"What's your unit, huh?" the doctor asked again.

A nurse bearing the rank of major walked over to the bedside.

"Let me see this patient, doctor," she said.

The nurse came over to Ronnie's bedside and waited for the doctor to withdraw.

"Hi sugar. I haven't gotten to meet you yet but let's get to know each other now. I'm Nurse Sandy, and I usually work in the psych ward. I just started my shift, so we'll have some time together. What's your name?"

"Ronnie."

"Hello Ronnie. What is your last name?"

"Stepovich."

"Good Ronnie. Do you know where you are?"

"I'm in a stinking hospital, but not for long."

"That's the spirit. Now, why don't you tell me how you got here?"

"I was in a town, in Fallujah, with a Marine Recon unit. We were providing security for a base and scouting out the bad guys in the town. We were playing cat and mouse with some sniper who got off a lucky shot. No, it wasn't all that lucky. I stuck my head out too many times and took a hit. After that I kind of remember being hauled downstairs and next thing I know, I'm here being accused of being a soldier named Gates. Can I have something to eat?"

The head surgeon looked at the empty bed where Ronnie Stepovich was supposed to be. "That guy is a pain in the butt," he said to himself. He put the guy on a regimen of strict bed rest. So, what did the guy do? He walked all over the ward, and nobody stopped him. The head surgeon changed the regimen to permit walking on this floor only. Then what? The guy walks down the stairs and uses the gym.

To the head surgeon, soldier Gates, who claimed to be a Marine by the name of Stepovich, was a serious problem. Not only had he, the head surgeon, pronounced the guy dead, but during his watch his staff had screwed up the identity of two patients, confusing Gates for Stepovich and vice versa. The surgeon was not convinced that Stepovich's mind was all there. The guy could not even remember what unit he was in! So maybe he really is Gates and the whole thing will blow over. If it doesn't, the possibility of this head surgeon ever getting a promotion is slim to none. "I liked this guy better when I thought he was dead," the surgeon mused to himself.

The surgeon put Ronnie in a psychiatric ward with no telephone access, and ordered a psychiatric workup so they could convince this guy that he really was Gates. Ronnie wasn't buying it.

At the moment, Ronnie wasn't in his bed because he was on an important reconnaissance mission involving stealing food from the food cart. The trick was to get the food out before the guy who was delivering could find out. The whole idea had come up when Ronnie told Nurse Sandy that they were starving him. She tried to order extra rations for him, but some goody two-shoes told the doctor about it and that plan was nixed. Then she told Ronnie to just steal some food from the food cart.

"I can't take some other guy's food," Ronnie objected.

"I'll order a meal for bed 409," she replied. "Nobody is in it, and the guy delivering the food won't notice where it goes if you can grab it while he's in one of the rooms. There is a female in room 407, and he always delays in the room while he drops the food off to her."

For frequently bucking the bureaucracy at the hospital, Nurse Sandy gained the everlasting gratitude of her patients. It also got her passed over for promotion to Lieutenant Colonel. What she did for patients was not always in line with what the brass wanted. Being stuck as a Major had its advantages. Higher promotions for her at this point would take her farther away from the patients that she wanted to work with. She was content.

Nobody in the hospital believed that Ronald Stepovich was in fact a Marine. He was supposed to be soldier Ronald Gates. That's what his dog tags said. Ronnie was comatose when Gates' dog tags were stuck on his gurney, so he wasn't in much of a position to correct the mistake. His dog tags had been removed from him in Fallujah because he was shot in the neck. Ronnie stayed comatose for two weeks while

Gates' misidentified body was sent back to the States and buried.

Nurse Sandy told the head surgeon that she believed the patient. She believed he really wasn't a soldier. The head surgeon ordered Nurse Sandy to "Leave this nut case alone and let the psychiatrist figure it out."

Nurse Sandy promptly thereafter made three phone calls. One call got her the phone number of the Commanding General's staff (Marines) in Fallujah. Call two got her the number of the personnel section for Marine Recon units in Fallujah. Call three got her the sergeant in Ronnie's former Recon unit. The men in his unit had been informed that his wounds were fatal, so they had not tried to get to the hospital.

"Holy smokes! Stinko's alive!" Sergeant Goya blurted out.

When the Sergeant told his Lieutenant, who couldn't repress a smile.

"Let's go see him!"

"Hi ya Sarge! Hey Lieutenant! How you doing?" Ronnie spotted them while he was eating lunch.

It occurred to Ronnie that recognition of his old comrades came right away.

"Stinko! Hey man, they told us you were dead!"

"Yeah, I was dead. They declared me dead, but some female doctor who wouldn't pay attention figured out differently and here I am."

"Do they really call you Gates?"

"Most of them do. They don't believe me. It might be helpful if you straighten them out."

"Well, geez, Stinko, you were worthless when you was alive so why should I try to bring you back to life? The Marine Corps will have to start paying you and everything."

"At this point I'd like to get my name back and get on a phone and call home."

"You haven't done that yet?"

"They won't give me a phone. They think I'm a nutcase."

"Well, sounds like they are doing good work here. They got you pegged. What do you think, Lieutenant?"

"He's joking, you know. Don't take the Sergeant seriously."

"Yeah, he is frickin hilarious. Hey, how are the guys doing? Is Greene OK?"

"Greene is out on a job. He doesn't even know you are alive."

"Did you get the sniper?"

"We haven't seen him or heard anything about him. Nothing. We haven't seen him for several weeks, since you were with us. Matter of fact, things have been quiet since you been gone."

"Guess I should stay gone. What did you do with my gear?"

"We shipped it home. Sorry man, we didn't know you would need them."

"It's OK. Guess I'm lucky to be breathing."

"How's the chow here?"

"It's OK, but I'm hungry all the time."

"Here, this might help."

The Sergeant slipped him a few candy bars and a flask with Jack Daniels.

"Take it easy with this until you know what you are doing."

"Now that's more like it!" Ronnie said enthusiastically.

After the Sergeant and the Lieutenant from his unit vouched for him, the Head Surgeon at the hospital took Ronnie out of the psych ward and gave him phone privileges. The first person he called was Jennifer, but she didn't answer. The next person he called was his mother. The surgeon had resigned himself to the fact that Ronnie was going to live and that he, the surgeon, was never going to see another promotion as long as he lived. At this point, he decided it was time to forget about figuring out ways for the guy to die accidentally and just help him out.

"Hello?"

"Is this Mrs. Stepovich?"

"Yes."

"Mrs. Stepovich, this is Doctor Dudley calling from the 28th Combat Support Hospital in Baghdad. Are you sitting down, Mrs. Stepovich? I have some news for you."

"I don't like it when the military calls me with news."

"Bear with me Mrs. Stepovich. Are you sitting down now?"

"Yes."

"OK, Mrs. Stepovich. There is someone who wants to talk to you."

"Mom?"

"Mom? This is Ronnie. I'm OK. I'm not dead."

Mom?

"Mom, say something."

"I need a cigarette."

Jennifer had been busy when she prepared the service for Ronnie's funeral. Mrs. Stepovich, Ronnie's mother, had requested that Jennifer make the arrangements. After the memorial service, Jennifer had been busy with her new job at the Speed Set Concrete factory. She had managed to compartmentalize her grief and just function. Stay plugged into the world. Don't zone out. She had re-hired Will Corning and Jean Patterson, former employees. She put Will Corning, the former office manager, in charge of general administrative operations and she put the factory supervisor in charge of production. Jean was in her former position in the office. Jennifer took a few days off after that.

Jennifer was tired of hearing people's condolences for the loss of her fiancé, Ronnie Stepovich. The ungrateful creep had died on her just when she needed him. Didn't even get a kid out of him! Runs off to do his patriotic duty. Ask not what your country can do for you! Ask what you can do for your country! Jesus, Ronnie. You could at least have knocked me up when you were on leave. Then at least I would have something left of you. Ronnie the prude. Other men? I'm not interested in other men. Other men don't do it for me.

From home Jennifer sent an email to Will Corning and Jean Patterson stating that she would be out for a while. Keep the place going.

She picked up a laptop and a good camera and went for a drive.

At first the supervisor of county roads in Lake County, Indiana, did not want to grant her a meeting. He begrudgingly acquiesced when Jennifer insisted. She told him that she could save him 15% of his budget. She arranged to meet him in his office spaces in a video room.

She started the brief with satellite photos of the county, a diagram of the county roads, the same diagram showing county roads with red highlights of spots that needed repair. She then displayed photos of one pothole after the next, photos of some cars with blown tires, and traffic jams. That only took four minutes.

"How does she do this stuff?" the country supervisor asked himself.

After generating a great deal of new business in northern Indiana, she was able to repeat the process in northern Illinois and southern Wisconsin. She explained to the clients that her quick-setting concrete could take an 18-wheeler in eight hours. Business became brisk.

While he was at the hospital, Ronnie's sergeant took measurements of his neck, chest, bicep, arm length, waist, hip, and inseam. Ronnie felt a little stupid while he took the measurements but the sarge told him to drink his Jack

Daniels and shut up. Sometimes you gotta do what you are told.

The Sergeant and the Lieutenant went over to the clothing store at the Baghdad exchange and ordered a full complement of every uniform that Ronnie was likely to need. His dress uniforms were shipped back home, but his work uniforms had been disposed of.

The Lieutenant put the bill on his credit card and figured his disbursing officer could figure out a way to pay him back. When they were done at the exchange they returned to the hospital and made copies of the receipts.

"Here, Stinko. Take this receipt to the exchange when they let you out and pick up your uniforms. And when you come back, don't die on us again, because you are causing a lot of trouble! And here's $50 bucks so you get the uniforms pressed. You don't want to look like a dip stick when you rise from the dead."

"I can't take your money."

"It's not my money, dip stick. It's Navy Relief money. Now take it."

It wasn't Navy Relief money because the Sergeant had not thought that far ahead. He just came up with that on the spur of the moment so Ronnie would not give him an argument.

Ronnie got a pass three days later to go to the exchange and pick up his uniforms. He also got running shoes and workout clothes. He was authorized to do that. He was not authorized to go to the enlisted club, but he did just that, where he ordered a giant steak with all the trimmings.

When he got back to the hospital, he put on his workout clothes and went to the weight room for two hours. He finished in time for the evening meal at the hospital.

Every chance he got he telephoned Jennifer. She did not answer.

A few days later Jennifer was back in her office at the factory when Jean Patterson walked in.

Have you seen this? Jean dropped a newspaper on Jennifer's desk.

Stepovich Lives!

"AP - Baghdad - Tales of his demise were greatly exaggerated. Corporal Ronald Stepovich, USMC, posthumous recipient of the Silver Star, was buried with honors four weeks ago in North Chicago. Now he is back from Iraq. He claims there was a mistake.

"The Army doctors declared me dead. I guess I was dead until one female doctor found a pulse. Then I was in a coma for two weeks while they buried Ronald Gates in my place."

This story was held until the Army notified the family of Specialist Ronald Gates. Our condolences go to the Gates family for the loss and for the terrible misunderstanding."

Stepovich stated "Gates and I came into the hospital at the same time. I had been shot in the neck and my dog tags were pulled off in Falllujah. We were medevacked to the

Army hospital in Baghdad and put in hospital gowns. When the hospital lost power, the lights went out for a while, and they accidentally put Gate's dog tags on my gurney. Then they thought that I was Gates and Gates was me."

"Corporal Stepovich says his biggest challenge now is to convince the Social Security Administration that he is still alive and breathing," The newspaper reported.

"They like me dead at Social Security. Stepovich said. They told me a couple of times that I'm dead."

The newspaper article continued:

"Ronnie 'The Rocket' Stepovich has been reported previously by this newspaper for being part of the National Champion Little League team, the State Champion baseball team with his high school team at North Chicago. He played varsity baseball in his first year at Northern Illinois University. While playing ball in college he reportedly got a walk while at bat, then stole second base, stole third base, and stole home. He received no fines or arrests for all the thieveries."

"He is known to his friends by the unusual moniker 'Stinko."

Jennifer read it twice. Jean had closed the door. Jennifer didn't know what to think. Her breathing was shallow. The door opened and in walked Ronnie Stepovich.

"Stepovich, are you for real?" Jennifer asked.

"Is that all you have to say? I called you about 30 times. What the heck?"

"We buried you."

"You must have done a lousy job of it. Here I am."

"I did a great job of it. There wasn't a dry eye in the place."

"Don't I even get a hug?"

"Ronnie, oh my God!"

She ran around the desk, and he ran to her. They collided in the middle.

The hug opened the waterworks for Jennifer. She sobbed. Ronnie just held her and couldn't talk.

"Ronnie! Sweetheart. Are you OK?"

"Yeah, I'm fine."

"Ronnie, is everything working on you?"

"You know Jennifer, that is not very subtle."

"To hell with subtle. How are you? Are you OK?"

"Yeah."

"OK, let's go."

"Go where?"

"Start a family."

"What? What about getting married first?"

"Get to that later."

"Don't you want to know what happened to me?"

She grabbed his hand and pulled him out the door.

"Later. Come on!"

They got to Jennifer's place in record time. They hugged and smooched for a couple of minutes. It was obvious that everything was working for Ronnie.

Things progressed wonderfully between them. Ronnie was reaching for a condom.

39

"What do you think you are doing?" Jennifer asked.

"What?"

"Ronnie, I want you."

"But I have to protect your virtue."

"My virtue? My VIRTUE? Stinko you bastard! I don't want MY VIRTUE. I want YOUR KID!"

Ronnie had always been sure he could understand women. It suddenly occurred to him that he may have been mistaken.

"What?"

"I want to get knocked up. I want your kid."

"Huh?"

"I want your kid. I want your flesh in my body, growing. I want to have something left from you the next time you leave me for godforsaken places."

"But I'm going to get out of the Corps and become a schoolteacher."

"Yeah, sure you are."

"That's the plan. That has always been the plan."

"I knew we would have this discussion. I just didn't think it would be now."

"What?"

"Ronnie, what have you talked about for the last four or five years?"

"Uh, you mean."

"Yeah, I mean Chesty Puller and five Navy Crosses, Smedley Butler and two Medals of Honor, Richard

Marcinko and Seal Team Six, Audie Murphy and winning every combat medal there is."

Stinko looked at her…

"The First Marine Division, Force Recon, the Army Airborne, the SEAL Teams, the fighter units of the Navy and Air Force, the GO TO units of the United States military!"

"Jennifer, you remember what I said?"

"Yes, dummy, I remember what you said. Stepovich, let's get serious. Tell me who the belligerents were in the Thirty Years' War. What effect did Bismarck have on Europe? What people were important to Queen Elizabeth I? How did the Treaty of Versailles set the stage for World War II?"

"Jennifer, you are making my pecker shrivel."

"Well, I'm not surprised. Do you know why you are good at Marine Recon?"

"I'm built for it."

"That's only part of it. How does a night patrol, deep in enemy territory sound to you?"

"Kind of cool."

"How about this? There is a long, incredibly hard patrol that gathers immensely important intelligence, that only a few men in the world can pull off. How does that sound?"

"REALLY COOL!"

"That's what I thought. I think you are getting hard again."

They slept for a bit. When he woke up Jennifer was looking into his eyes.

"Are you for real?"

"Huh?"

"Are you for real?"

"What?" He was confused.

"Ronnie! What the hell?" She almost shouted. "You didn't write! You didn't phone! Not even an email! Is that how you treat someone you love?"

"I uh, uh…"

"You what? You are alive. Can't you pick up the phone? What happened?"

"I was in Iraq, you know."

"Yeah, I know. And?"

"I got shot."

She could see the scar on his neck.

"I was in a coma, and they confused me for another guy and declared me dead. Only I wasn't dead."

"You were dead. We buried you."

"Did I get a funeral?"

"Yeah, we gave you a funeral you jerk! You were dead. What do you expect?"

"Well, I'm not dead now."

"You are gonna be dead if you pull this again! Well, what happened after that?"

"I kept telling them that my name was Stepovich and not Gates. They thought I was loony, so they put me in a psych ward and took away my telephone privileges."

"I was kind of groggy but could still do stuff like ride a bicycle indoors in the hospital."

"That sounds right. Ronnie Stepovich, still exercising even when his brain stopped."

"So, after I convinced the doctors and nurses that I am who I am, they flew me to a hospital in Germany where this incredibly cool sergeant got me a flight back home and gave me her credit card. Can you believe that?"

"This sergeant is a SHE? Stepovich, what am I going to do with you?"

Ronnie spent three days with Jennifer. During the two days they visited his mother and had dinner with her. Mostly Ron and Jen just hung out.

"Jen, I always figured I'd get out after this tour in the Marine Corps and become a history teacher."

"Are we back on that again? Jennifer asked. Does being a history teacher feel right to you?"

"I don't know."

"What have you done to prepare for that?"

This drew a blank look.

"I suspect you were meant for something else."

"Meant for something?"

"What do you feel in your gut is right for you?"

"I don't know."

"You wrote me. Before all this. I read your letters. When you were gone, that was all I had left of you. I read them lots of times."

She paused for a few seconds then asked, "Who are the people you most admire?"

"Well, that would be Jack, Gino the coach, the Sergeant

Major who got me into Recon, the Lieutenant I used to work out with."

"OK, why Jack?"

"Jack got me out of my shell. He got me into doing sports seriously and realizing I could make a difference."

"Why Gino?"

"He developed me. He developed everyone in ways you wouldn't believe. He could bring out what is good in anybody. He just happens to be a baseball coach."

"Tell me some of the things you have done that you really enjoyed."

"I enjoyed the evasion course we did in boot camp. This guy we called 'The Walrus' and I made it to Freedom Village twice when nobody else did."

"I enjoyed field maneuvers when I got into Force Recon."

"I was scared out of my wits, but I enjoyed the first days in Iraq when we secured the oil rigs before the Iraqi forces could blow them up. The Sergeant and the Lieutenant that I worked with said my suggestions helped them out a lot."

"I enjoyed the camaraderie in the Corps. I liked the guys I served with."

"You haven't mentioned how you loved reading any history books."

"But service in the Corps will mean separations."

"Ronnie, at the end of the day, when the sun goes down, I want to see you across the dinner table from me. When evening comes nothing would make me happier than seeing you in the room with me. But I'm not willing to chain you down to get that. You have to do what feels right for you."

After a few days Ronnie figured it was time to come back to life officially. He telephoned the IRS, where a guy named Irving answered the phone. Irving was irritated.

He had been with the IRS for one year. Irving wanted a government job because he wanted the most security possible that went along with the least amount of work. Irving was totally disillusioned with the IRS. As far as he was concerned, the IRS was not the place for him because there was a lot of work. Lately it seemed everything he did turned into a can of worms. If he was rude to a customer, his boss saw it. If he made an entry error, his boss caught it. If he grumbled in front of a customer, his boss gave him a lecture. The workload piled up. Today the office was jammed with people waiting to be seen. The phone rang. Irving was the bottom man on the totem pole, so he had to answer the phone.

The guy on the phone said, "This is Ronnie Stepovich. I am with the U.S. Marine Corps. I was mistakenly identified as being KIA in Iraq and I want to make sure your records are straight."

By KIA Irving assumed the guy meant Killed in Action.

"OK. Give me your SSN and I'll call you up."

Ronnie provided the number.

"It says here you are deceased."

"That is wrong as you can tell because I am talking to you."

"I don't know who you are buddy, but you got a sick sense of humor."

Irving hung up the phone and hoped the problem would go away.

The phone rang again.

"This is me again, Ronnie Stepovich. I'm not dead."

"OK, let me check with my supervisor."

Ronnie was on hold for a long time. The supervisor was busy, and Irving knew that he would be verbally abused if he interrupted the supervisor. After a while Irving returned to the phone.

"Hello, you there? Come in and fill out a form."

"What form? Ronnie asked."

It was too late. Irving had already hung up.

Ronnie took a number at the IRS counter and waited his turn. When his number came up, he was greeted by none other than Irving of the IRS.

"I'm Ronnie Stepovich. I need to re-establish by Social Security Number because I was mistakenly identified as killed while I was serving in Iraq."

"Let me see a picture ID, your birth certificate, and your Social Security card, please."

Ronnie produced the requested items.

"Your driver license is expired."

"I was serving in Iraq when it expired. I'll get it updated." Ronnie didn't explain that his real license was lost in Iraq, and he had brought in his old one.

Irving brought his supervisor over because this was an unusual circumstance.

"Please fill out this form, Mr. Stepovich, and explain the circumstances."

Ronnie filled out the form and turned it in.

"When can I expect to hear from you?"

"Call back in a week. We should know something by then."

A week later Ronnie called and got to speak to Irving after only one ring.

"Oh, Mr. Stepovich? Yes. I have something here. It says, it says... Did you ever have Social Security wages, Mr. Stepovich?"

"Did I have Social Security wages? Yes, I worked two summers in a factory and had five years in the Marine Corps. I have statements from the Social Security Administration showing the annual amounts. They are at home."

"Well, you have no record of Social Security wages at all. Are you sure you gave us the correct Social Security Number?"

"Yes."

"My supervisor says you should give us a statement of your work history. We are going to research it for you."

Ronnie returned the next day with a briefcase full of documents and a pocket full of ID. He met one more time with the supervisor at Social Security. He got the feeling he was trying to make water flow uphill.

He went home with all the documents that were with him.

"How did it go?" His mother asked.

"Not well." He explained what happened.

"Speak to Gino."

"Gino? He's a baseball coach. He's a cook who owns a restaurant. How would that help?"

"Gino knows everybody."

"So?"

"You can't get past this supervisor? Try an end run."

"Huh?"

"You think only in terms of baseball? It's a football term."

Mothers can be frustrating.

"I know this, Mom. How can Gino help?"

"He'll know someone at the IRS who can fix it."

Ronnie looked perplexed.

"By fix it I don't mean bribe the guy. I mean fix the problem and get you set up again."

"Mom, I might have gotten dead. I didn't get stupid. I know what you mean."

Gino did know someone at the IRS. The person he knew was a Database Administrator (DBA), who maintained some of the databases. Gino gave her phone number to Ronnie. He called her number.

"Meet me for lunch where we can talk." The DBA did not trust government telephones and didn't want to talk where the wrong person could hear.

The DBA had a kid who played on Gino's baseball teams. She recognized Ronnie.

They ordered lunch. The DBA asked to see his Social Security Card and some of his Marine Corps pay slips. At that point she was certain that Ronnie had given him the correct SSN, and that her research had been for that SSN.

The DBA explained the situation.

"I've checked our records. Your SSN is out of our system. I don't know how that happened. I reloaded some of our backup tapes from a couple of years back and they are damaged. You know, unreadable. The tapes are curled or something. Sometimes that happens. I can get your data back in again, no problem, but I don't have your financial data for the five plus years that you worked."

"I have the annual records, would that help?"

"It would help. I can re-enter your records for each payday, but I would need the dates, amounts, and the Employer ID number for each transaction. That is a lot of data entry. Probably 26 paydays per year for five years, but it can be done. Unless…"

"Unless what?"

"Ronnie, you went into the Marine Corps the same time that Jack Russell did, right?"

"Yeah. We joined up at the same time and started active duty when we went to boot camp the same day. Our pay records are the same until this year, except for the unit I was in."

The DBA said, "You had some combat pay that he may

not have, but close enough. I can copy his pay dates, pay amounts, and employer ID into records for your SSN with just a couple of SQL statements. That will only take a few minutes. I can change the employer ID later."

"We worked in the cement factory on the same dates too. That was for two summers," Ronnie said.

"After you did boot camp, give me the title of each outfit you were with and the dates as well as you can remember them. We can get the Employer ID number if we have the title of the organization," the DBA explained. "It really won't upset anybody to put this data in. I'll make the annual amounts match your totals from your annual statement that you have here in paper copy. If there are any modifications that need to be made later, they will be very minor."

"I don't know how to thank you."

"You already have, by your service."

Chapter 4

A Farm near Kandahar, Afghanistan

As Abdul and Meena walked through the night toward the barn, the strong wind almost knocked them off their feet. In a moment they were chilled to the bone. They opened the barn door and located the generator. Meena threw the switches and started the generator. In a moment the barn was filled with a dull light.

Abdul had been on the farm for several weeks, during which time they had planted the seeds for the spring wheat, then they pulled some rocks out of the fields. He had picked up more rocks than he thought was possible in four lifetimes. Meena looked at him strangely.

"Abdul, I'm engaged and I'm out here alone in this barn with you at night. This won't look good."

Abdul thought of the last time they had been alone in this barn together. That was more than a year ago, and they had kissed, over there, by the tractor. He had thought of that moment six thousand times since then. Now she was engaged to someone else.

"Meena, you trust me, don't you?"

She looked at him and said nothing.

"Abdul, my boy," he said to himself., "you do have a way with women."

"Of course, you trust me!" he said. "Why else would you be out here at night?"

She continued her silence.

"OK, let's get going!" he said.

Abdul grabbed the first bale of hay and placed it where he wanted it. He put another on top of it.

"Are you going to stand there like a queen or are you going to do something?" he asked.

Meena pulled a bale off the wall and asked, "Where do you want it?"

"Put down a row here, five meters long. He pointed in the direction he wanted the bales. Then we will put down another row two meters from it, parallel to the first one. Then we will stack the bales on top until it is as high as either of us can reach."

They made two parallel rows of bales, a little over six feet apart, and sixteen feet long. After stacking the last row up to a height of eight feet, they put spare metal barn siding on top the bales. He then grabbed a ladder and put bales of hay on top of the metal roof he had created. When that was done, he put a wall on the back end so that entry was only possible from the front.

"You built a sound chamber. It won't be soundproof, you know. What are you going to do, rip my clothes off and rape me?"

He looked her in the eye. "In my dreams maybe. Now we are going to practice."

"Practice? Practice what?" Meena asked.

Abdul pulled a coin out of his pocket, about one inch in

diameter. He placed it at eye height on one of the bales of hay at the back end. He and Meena walked to the front end.

"Now the work begins," he said.

"Oh, what we did before was not work?"

"No, that was all preparation, and it was necessary, but that wasn't the work. Now the work begins."

"What are you talking about?"

Abdul pulled a pistol out of his clothing. "Come here."

"Where did you get that?"

"Your father."

"My father gave you that? Where did he get it?"

"He bought it on the black market in town. This isn't the only one."

"What are we going to do with it?"

"When the Taliban come at harvest time to steal your crop, you will be ready."

"With a pistol?"

"They won't expect you to have it. That is why it will work."

"So, you are going to have me shoot holes in coins for the next few months? Abdul, you are brilliant."

"You don't get to shoot bullets tonight. Tonight, you just sight in. Even the coin is safe tonight. Not that you could hit it."

She stared at him. "Keep talking Abdul. I'll shoot something on your body that will make you shut up."

Abdul looked at her in surprise and the same thought

came back to haunt him. Yes, Abdul, you do have a way with the women.

Abdul sat at the kitchen table with Meena and her father, Wasim.

"We are going to have to explain your presence here," Wasim said. "For the last month nobody outside of the family saw you, we will have visitors coming this weekend. Meena's fiancé will visit with her family."

Abdul knew this fiancé would show up sooner or later.

"OK, what do you suggest?"

"How can we explain that you have been staying here for months? Should we say you are a hired gun to protect us from thieves?"

It was too close to the truth for Abdul. He was wanted in Iraq and did not want to get the word out that he was good with a gun.

"No. It has to be something else," Abdul said.

"You are my sister's son," Wasim said.

"You never talked about your sister, Dad. You don't have one," Meena retorted.

"That's because she was an illegitimate child," Wasim replied as he made up the story. "The family hid her existence. Yes, Abdul is the bastard son of an illegitimate sister of mine."

"This is getting better and better," Abdul replied.

"If you make it too salacious, tongues will wag," Meena said.

Eyebrows went up. "Where did you get that word?" her father asked.

"From the trashy novels that Mom reads."

"She isn't the only one reading them, obviously," her father replied.

Meena replied, "His story had better be boring or it will be told and retold. It should be routine."

"OK. My sister was promised in marriage at a very early age. She left the family at the age of 13 and has lived far away ever since."

"I don't have a local accent," Abdul replied. "I won't learn the local accent in the next few weeks either. I can pass as an Iraqi because that is what I am. My mother lived in Iraq."

"Then why did you come here? What is your story?"

"I lost my job in construction."

"Why did you lose your job? Downturn in the economy?" Meena asked.

"No, everyone knows the Americans will pay to build anything. Getting a job is too easy," Wasim replied. "Abdul lost his job because he is unreliable. He was fired from two jobs because he didn't show up for work. He had a drinking problem. He left the true faith and took to drinking."

"OK, I'm the nephew who came here because I couldn't hold a job at home. My mother could not support me, and my father died when I was young. My career was in building construction. I was a laborer."

"I liked it better when you were the bastard son of my

illegitimate sister," Wasim said. "But I can live with it. You are my nephew, son of my sister, and you are an unreliable laborer who had a drinking problem."

"How long am I staying with you?" Abdul asked. His heart beat fast when he asked the question.

"None of us know," Father Wasim replied.

They discussed Abdul's alibi again the next night. They agreed that his story would be that he was the son of Wasim's sister who lived in Kabul, the capital of Afghanistan. Abdul had a bad accent because he was not right in the head. He couldn't remember Kabul, also because he was not right in the head. He had never held any job other than laborer, and he could not hold jobs for long because of his drinking binges. He was an unreliable laborer. He did better on the farm because there was no alcohol here and Wasim was strict with him. That was the story they agreed upon.

The crops were in the ground and growing. The time finally came when Meena's fiancé and his family would visit her on her farm. The fiancé's name was Bahraam, and Abdul thought that he was not particularly good looking. Of course, it did not matter what he thought. It mattered a great deal what Meena thought and what her parents thought.

Abdul was aware that Bahraam and Meena were never allowed to be alone together. That was a stark contrast to the way Abdul was treated by Meena's family. He and Meena were alone together a lot of the time. They worked alone in the fields together for the past few weeks.

Abdul was uncomfortable being in the same room as

Bahraam. As soon as dinner was over, Abdul found an excuse to leave the group. Bahraam did not feel threatened by Abdul because it was explained that Abdul was simple in the head, couldn't remember much, and spoke poorly. Abdul was quiet most of the time. When night fell Bahraam and his family got on the family truck and went back to their own farm. Abdul went out to the barn and was surprised to see Meena join him.

"I'm surprised to see you here," Abdul said.

"I wanted to practice some."

"OK."

Abdul got the pistol out of the locked box that was chained to a post in the barn.

"What do you want to work on tonight?"

Meena had learned to shoot combat style. They practiced starting with the pistol in the hand pointed at the ground and the arms hanging loosely at the side. The method was to raise the weapon smoothly using only one hand, point, and shoot. Another type of shooting is slow fire, with careful sighting and two-handed shooting, allowing a few seconds per shot.

"Let's start with combat range."

They did some dry firing for a while. After that they added two bullets to the weapon. Abdul put up a piece of paper with a black circle in the center. She put both shots in the black.

Abdul drew another target on a piece of paper. This one had a small white circle on the inside of a black bull eye.

"Try hitting that."

Slow fire, right?

"OK."

She first sighted with an unloaded weapon. Abdul watched.

"Get behind me," she said.

He did.

"Help me hold the weapon."

She didn't need help holding the weapon and they both knew it.

It was a quiet night. The air was dead calm. They were inside the rows of hay bales. It was dead silent. Abdul stood behind her and pressed up against her body. She pulled her head covering down and raised her hands with the pistol. He reached around her and held her arms in position. His cheek was pressed against hers. He could feel her rear end pressing into him. He could smell the sweetness of her hair. They held the position for a minute then without a word lowered their hands. He was still behind her. He wrapped his arms around her and held her. She slowly stroked his hand.

"Why did you come back, Abdul?"

He thought of teasing her by saying how much he enjoyed the soil and the sun, but he had spent too many months in agony to tell her a lie.

"I… came back for you."

"I hoped you would say that." She turned around and kissed him.

When the spring wheat was ready for harvest, it was

well into the fall. Meena's father Wasim and Abdul went to Bahraam's farm for two days to help with the harvest. The previous generation had done this job with a scythe and a flat wagon pulled by mules, but this generation used dump trucks and a combine that the neighboring farmers shared. The combine whacked the wheat and dumped the wheat into the dump truck via a twenty-foot-long spout. The combine driver and truck driver had to match each other's speed, so they stayed together. The job could have been completed in less time if the combine hadn't needed frequent repairs.

After the wheat was harvested on Bahraam's farm they all moved to Wasim's farm to collect the wheat there. Father Wasim had daughters and no sons, which made his farm a likelier target for thieves. They nearly completed the harvest when they saw three trucks approaching on the long road that led into the farm. Each vehicle was a flatbed truck with a driver and three men standing in the bed behind the cab, holding rifles across their chests. Abdul ran to the cab of the truck where he was working and pulled out a rifle with a scope.

"Abdul, what are you doing?" Bahraam asked.

Father Wasim spoke to Bahraam in a hushed voice.

"Let him work, Bahraam."

"But he's a simpleton! He'll get us all killed!"

"Shut up Bahraam!"

Abdul had observed the wind that day. He got into a position on his stomach, flat on the ground, spread his legs, and sighted in. When the lead truck was at 800 meters Abdul fired his first shot. The front tire on the driver's side took the hit and went flat. The truck slowed down but did not stop. Abdul shot out the other tire with his second shot.

"Are you going to let him do this?" Bahraam shouted.

"Bahraam, I said shut up!" Wasim shouted back.

Father Wasim pulled another rifle out of the cab of the truck and stood behind the engine. He had a good firing position over the hood of the truck. Neither the engine nor the hood of the truck was hot.

The thieves in the bed of the lead truck began firing. From 800 meters in a moving truck on a rough road there was little chance they would hit anything. Wasim held his fire and waited.

"Get behind the engine of the truck you idiot!" Wasim shouted at Bahraam. "Get down!"

The lead truck was still moving forward, but very slowly due to the flat tires. The bandits were shooting, then ducking down behind the cab, then popping up and shooting again. Abdul watched the men in the truck. The man in the center of the three who stood behind the cab of the lead truck popped up from the same position twice in a row. The third time he popped up Abdul put a bullet in his chest. Abdul put a bullet through the front window, killing the driver. The truck came to a stop. The second truck pulled around the first truck. Abdul's first shot at truck number two appeared to be a miss. His second shot hit one of the men behind the cab who had exposed himself.

"Abdul! The tires!" Wasim shouted at him.

Abdul took aim and hit the front tire on the driver's side of truck number two. The truck kept coming. He shot out the other tire. The truck kept coming slowly. The first truck had a dead driver, so the men abandoned that truck and now walked behind truck number two. The third truck stayed thirty meters back and came to a stop.

At four hundred meters Abdul was able to kill one of the men who stood behind the cab of the truck. Only one truck kept coming. There was now one man in the bed of the truck and one very clever driver who stayed down. How he could see to control the truck they couldn't guess.

Wasim started firing when the distance to the approaching truck was 300 meters. He shot into the truck's radiator and put another shot into the radiator of the third truck that was well behind it. After that he fired rapidly, hoping that his volume of fire would discourage the enemy. For a while nobody presented a target as the truck crept up. There was a moment of quiet that was broken when shots erupted in rapid succession from the house behind them. There was a bandit on the porch of the house, and he held one of the daughters as a hostage. Wasim shouted a curse.

Two men who walked behind the truck exposed themselves to attempt a shot. Abdul put a bullet into the chest of both of them.

"Abdul you bastard! Stop firing!" Bahraam shouted. "They will kill the women!"

There was shouting from the porch of the house.

The last man on the bed of the truck stood up and fired. Abdul killed him with a head shot. The truck driver drove straight at Abdul and would have driven over him except Abdul rolled between the wheels at the last second. The truck passed over him then stopped abruptly and backed up. Abdul ran to the passenger's side, jumped up on the running board and jammed the rifle into the cab and shot three times in rapid fire into the driver's body. Abdul climbed into the cab and stuck his rifle into the driver's ear.

"Who is your leader?" Abdul shouted. "Who?"

"Borst. His name is Borst."

"Where is he? Where is Borst?"

"The last truck." It was the last thing the driver said before dying from his wounds.

The last truck and the bandit leader Borst with it had made a U turn and left the area when the fighting started.

"Abdul you bastard! They will kill the women!" Bahraam shouted.

Wasim was running at a sprint toward his home. One of his daughters had been clubbed on the head with a pistol and was passed out on the front porch. His wife was bleeding from a gash in the face. The bandit on the porch held Meena's mother from behind. One shot was heard from inside the house, then another. The mother screamed. "Oh my God! Oh my God! Meena! Meena!"

Meena burst through the front door.

"My God! What are you doing? What are you doing?" Meena shouted. "What have you done?"

"Shut up bitch!" The bandit who held her mother shouted right back.

"Look at this!" Meena shouted and waived her left hand. She raised a pistol with her right hand from behind her skirt and shot the bandit in the face.

Meena's mother ran over to her daughter who was still unconscious on the porch.

Meena shouted. "Abdul!"

Abdul and Wasim ran up to the porch.

"Abdul! There is a man still in the house. I shot him but he might still be alive!" Meena shouted.

"Get away from the house!" Abdul shouted at Wasim.

"It's my home!" Father Wasim shouted.

"Yes!" Abdul shouted right back. "Don't get killed in it!"

"All of you get in the barn!" Abdul shouted. "Wasim and I will watch the doors."

"What now, Abdul?" Wasim asked.

"We take a position so we can shoot without hitting each other. You watch the front door. I'll watch the back. We watch the doors and listen. If anyone is alive, we shoot them when they come out of the house. None of the family is in the house. They are all out here. So, don't run into the house and get shot. Do you understand? Meena, get in the barn and stay there! Take the first aid kit out of this truck and do what you can about your mother's injury."

Meena gave the first aid kit to her mother. Bahraam and Meena carried her sister to the barn. Her mother was right behind them.

Abdul and Wasim waited outside the house for several minutes, but nobody came out of the house.

"Wasim! Stay there! I'll go in the house and check!"

Abdul snuck into the house from the back and searched each room. The man was still there where Meena had left him, dead.

Abdul opened a window and shouted, "All Clear! All Clear! I'm going to come out the front door, do not shoot! Do not shoot! It's me! Abdul!"

He then walked out the front door and shouted, "Let's check the men in the fields!"

Eight men had come in the first two trucks, arriving by the road that led to the front door of the farmhouse. Two men had entered the house from the rear and surprised the women inside. Abdul didn't know how the two men had arrived at the farm, because they weren't in the trucks that came down the road. One of the men had gone through the house to the front porch, where he clubbed the sister and grabbed the mother. Meena's sister appeared to have a concussion and her mother had a scar on the face that would require stitches and antibiotics.

They examined the bodies in the fields and trucks one by one. Bahraam was throwing up. Abdul examined each one calmly while pointing a rifle at them.

When he stopped puking, Bahraam looked at Abdul. "You have done this before?" Bahraam asked Abdul.

Abdul looked at him and kept walking.

"You aren't what you said you were," Bahraam said.

"You aren't what you said you were!" Bahraam repeated. "You aren't the nephew either, are you?"

Abdul did not reply. Meena ran up to Abdul and wrapped her arms around him.

Wasim wanted to get a doctor to come to his house. He got into his truck and drove down the road that led away from his house. The potholes were deep so he could not drive quickly. He knew he was in trouble when he had driven over the hill and saw the men behind the rocks pointing rifles at him. The men with rifles jumped out from behind the rocks and blocked the path of his truck. Wasim stopped the truck and reached for his rifle, but he could not bring it to bear quickly. The men had their weapons pointed at him.

The bandit leader jammed a rifle in his ear. "Get out of the truck!"

"Why? I have done nothing."

"Get out now or we'll shoot you! Get out now you dog!"

Wasim acquiesced.

Wasim noticed that their truck's radiator had a hole in it. That was from his shot earlier.

"Turn around and walk!"

Wasim hesitated.

Blam! The bandit leader fired a shot into the ground at Wasim's feet.

Blam! "Walk!"

Wasim took a few steps as Borst and his man climbed into Wasim's truck and sped away.

Police in the area were non-existent.

Chapter 5

Camp Dwyer, Afghanistan

Sergeant Major James Johnson, United States Marine Corps, was an unusual man. None of the people who knew him during his first days in the Corps could understand why he got promoted to the rank he now held, the highest possible rank an enlisted man can hold.

Johnson used to joke with his friends by saying "You know how every time the advancement lists come out and there is one guy on the list, and everyone says, 'How did that asshole get promoted?' I want to be that asshole!"

Every time that Johnson met the time in grade requirement and the advancement list came out, there was James Johnson's name on it. Johnson wasn't the brightest guy you ever met, nor was he the greatest leader. But during every foreign assignment that Johnson had, he learned the local language.

"Holy Smokes!" Sergeant Major Johnson exclaimed as he sat in a small office in the middle of Afghanistan and read the daily intelligence summary.

"What is it?" Lieutenant Ernst Gilmere asked.

"It says here that twelve men armed with rifles attacked the family of a wheat farmer who had two daughters. The twelve men were all killed, and the farmer and his daughters

67

survived, with minor injuries. What the …. It says the farmer had the help of one man who lives with them and is believed to be the son in law. I don't get it."

"What's to get?"

"How can one man and a farmer take out 12 armed men? We have been trying to subdue the Taliban for six years now. We have had limited success. I have got to meet this farmer guy and this gunslinger son in law."

The farm was farther away than they expected. The roads in the country did not allow rapid driving, so when they arrived, it was in the afternoon. They brought an interpreter, although Johnson could have done the job himself.

The Sergeant Major stopped his convoy of three Humvees a few miles short of the farm.

He gave specific directions to his men: "When we get to this place, we drive in with helmets and flak jackets on. Nobody, and I mean nobody, lifts a weapon unless I say so. The people who live here are obviously good shooters, so give them no reason to start shooting. Keep your weapons down, your eyes open and your mouth shut. Got that? Weapons down!"

Corporal John Rogers realized that Lieutenant Gilmere outranked everyone in this detail, but the Sergeant Major was the real leader, and everyone knew it. Rogers could have given the Sergeant Major's brief himself: "Keep your mouth shut, your eyes open, and don't screw up." The Sergeant Major's speeches were predictable.

They drove down the road that led up to the farm. The road went over a hill then made a gentle curve and passed a big rock that was painted white. One hundred yards later was another rock, also white. A hundred yards after that was a large rock, painted red. One hundred yards later was another red rock. That makes two white and two red, Corporal Rogers observed. After that the pattern repeated itself.

They drove up to the farmhouse. Father Wasim walked onto the porch to meet them. Lieutenant Gilmere was relieved to see that the farmer carried no weapon.

"What can I do for you gentlemen?" Wasim asked.

"Are you the man who defended this place against 12 men with rifles?"

"No."

"Is this the place that was attacked by the Taliban not long ago?"

"Why do you ask?"

"So, who defended it?"

There was hesitation, but Wasim answered, "That would be Abdul."

"Abdul? Is he your son in law?"

"No."

"Who is he?"

"I'll get him for you. He can explain for himself."

Wasim was afraid he would say something to get Abdul in trouble.

When Abdul saw the American vehicles approaching, he left the field and drove Wasim's truck back to the farmhouse. He had his hand on the rifle, but when he saw that none of the Americans carried a weapon, he left the rifle in the truck. Wasim asked Abdul to join the group.

"Are you the man who defended the farm from 12 men here last week?" The Sergeant Major worked through an interpreter.

"No sir.

"You didn't? Who did?"

"There weren't 12 men here."

"How many were there?"

"Ten."

"That's all? Did you kill the 10 men?"

"No sir."

"Could you explain what happened?"

"We live on a farm here. We raise wheat. Last year some men came and stole the whole harvest before Wasim could sell it. This year these men came with large trucks, big enough to carry our entire harvest of wheat. They carried rifles. I shot out one of their tires. They could have stopped, but they didn't. They started shooting and kept coming at us. They were shooting rifles. At us! Farmers! At that point I figured their intention was to kill us or steal our wheat, so I started to defend our farm."

"When did you start shooting?"

"When the trucks were down the road."

"What do you mean?"

Abdul recognized that the man asking the questions was a Marine because of his globe and anchor. Abdul had memorized Marine insignia when he had been in Baghdad. He also recognized that the Marine was a Sergeant Major. Abdul realized it would be a very bad idea to let the American know that he knew this much about them, because it would reveal the fact that Abdul had fought Marines before.

Abdul addressed the interpreter, "Tell this man that we were willing to live in peace, but these men came here and started shooting at us. They also had two men who snuck around the back of the house, entered the house, and tried to rape our women."

"What happened to them?"

"They were shot."

"Who shot them?"

"One of the women that they molested."

"Who?"

"A daughter."

"What did she have to defend herself?"

"A pistol."

"How is it that an Afghani woman knows how to use a pistol?"

"After the farm was attacked last year and the whole crop was stolen, Father Wasim bought a pistol. She must have figured out how to use it."

"How many men were inside the house?"

71

"Two."

"And they were both shot? Killed? In the house?"

"One was killed in the house. One was killed on the porch when he beat up the mother and daughter."

"So, there were eight men outside the house, is that correct?"

"Yes."

"And you shot them. How?"

"They shot at me, so I shot back. If I hadn't, we all would be dead, and the crop stolen, again, like it was last year."

The Sergeant Major looked at Lieutenant Gilmere and said, "I still don't get it. How could one guy hold this place against eight men?"

"Good question," the Lieutenant replied.

Breaking the admonition to keep his mouth shut, Corporal Rogers piped up and said, "This place is a rifle range."

The Sergeant Major didn't expect input from the peanut gallery, but he had learned from experience to listen to his people.

"What was that Corporal?"

"We are standing on a rifle range, Sergeant Major. You could see it as we drove up."

"Explain yourself."

"We are on the porch of this farm. Do you see the road we drove up as we came in? Do you see those big rocks that are evenly spaced? Do you see that they are painted? I'll bet we could pace off the distance to them and find they are at 100-meter intervals, not from each other but from this porch. I'll bet that great big rock in the front yard is not out there by coincidence. I'll bet it is the firing position this guy used."

Sergeant Major Johnson realized he was looking at a truly skillful fighter.

"What weapon did you use?"

Abdul was afraid they would take his rifle with the scope.

"Is that what you came here to talk about? Guns?" Abdul asked in reply.

"As a matter of fact, it is not what I came to talk about. I came to talk about a better land, a land free of thieves who take a man's crop, who take a man's life's work, who just about take the food off his table, who come to attack his farm and his wife and his family. We can have a better land than that."

"How long will you be here, in this land?" Abdul asked. "Why should I talk to you? You will leave. The Taliban will come back."

"They may come back, but you are not alone. You have neighbors and in time your government will help you."

Father Wasim spoke up now. "The neighbors are no help. They do what the Taliban says, and the Taliban always come back."

"The Taliban are like all men. They follow leaders. Right now, they follow the bandit leader named Borst" the Sergeant Major said.

Wasim knew Borst. Too well.

"So, what do you plan to do about Borst?"

"We will find him."

Wasim said, "That will not be easy."

Chapter 6

Bandit leader Borst was furious with Wasim. Borst had never lost men before. Borst had a reputation for always succeeding. Borst took care of his men. Borst was always lucky. Wasim had ruined all that. Now recruiting had ground to a halt. His band had lost too many men on Wasim's farm. Who was the unknown marksman, and how could his men have been killed inside the farmhouse? Women! Killed by women!

Borst had to prove himself to his Taliban tribe. He would show them. He was someone to be respected and feared!

Borst hated Wasim even before the debacle on the farm. Borst hated Wasim because Wasim made tractors run. Not just for a day or two, he made them run year after year. He made his trucks run. It's not easy to do. Borst had tried that, and it never worked for him.

The bandit leader Borst was well-concealed behind rocks beside the highway. His five men had been waiting for hours. They saw Wasim leave the farm in his truck. They saw Wasim's truck winding down the road as it approached. At his instruction, Borst's men had rolled large rocks into the road at a point just over the crest of a hill. Wasim would not see the rocks until it was too late. His speed was down to a crawl as he climbed the hill because large ruts had formed in the dirt road.

Wasim had gone to town to sell wheat. He had driven a truck that he had bought to replace the one that Borst had stolen. He got a fair price for the wheat and picked up some things in town. Wasim drove up the hill slowly and did not suspect a thing. He cursed when he saw the rocks in the road. Borst and four other men leaped from behind the boulder and pointed their rifles at him.

"Do what I say, or you are a dead man! Get out of the truck!"

Father Wasim had to comply.

"Kneel! Search him!"

They found a substantial amount of money on Wasim, along with a necklace that Wasim had bought for his wife.

"He's got a rifle in the truck!"

Borst hit Wasim in the back of the head with the butt of a rifle.

Wasim fell face down unconscious on the dry ground and broke his nose. When he regained consciousness his truck, his money, and the necklace were gone.

Sergeant Major James Johnson, United States Marine Corps, returned to Wasim's farm within the week. He asked Wasim and his family to come together. He asked that Abdul be included in the meeting. He introduced himself once again. He began to speak in Dari, the predominant language of Afghanistan. It was a while before he allowed his interpreter to take over and read the proposal that he had written. This proposal had gotten approval from military and agency leaders.

The proposal stated, "We are aware of the problems that your family has experienced with the Taliban. We believe that these problems will continue. There may be something we can do to help you. However, you must agree to it, and Abdul also must agree to it. This is the offer. Abdul works with us to capture or kill Borst. That may remove your problem with the Taliban temporarily, but we do not believe that it will work permanently. So, we can bring your family to the United States. We have agreement from the United States Department of State and the INS, the Immigration and Naturalization Service, to do this. You and your family can move to a city or to a farm in the United States. You can raise wheat, corn, barley, soybeans, whatever you want. You will be able to sell your farm here before you go. Your story will be that you are moving to Kabul, or a town near Kabul, to repair tractors and trucks, and you are taking your family with you. Abdul will work with us to get rid of Borst. Abdul will be paid for his work. If he wishes, Abdul will be able to live wherever he chooses when the work is done."

"If you are interested in this, we will provide pictures of the farm in the United States. There is a home with four bedrooms, electricity, and running water. There are people in the area who speak your language. There will be people to help you to learn English. There is a mosque, but it is about 30 minutes away. You can choose this farm, or you can choose another. It is your decision."

"Is the mosque Shia or Sunni?" Wasim asked the Sergeant Major.

"I don't know. I will find out," the Sergeant Major replied in Dari.

"Will there be some money to buy seeds so we can get started?"

"Yes. I already know that."

"Can my daughters attend school?"

"Yes. In fact, in the United States more than half the students in universities are women."

"Can my daughters study international affairs if they want?"

"Yes."

"Can my daughters study computers if they want?"

"Yes."

"Can I become a citizen of the United States?"

"Yes."

"Do I have to become a citizen of the United States?"

"No. It is your choice."

"Can my wife attend school?"

"Yes. She can study in a school, or she can study at home with a tutor, or both. An instructor who is a woman can help her."

"Can Abdul become a citizen of the Unites States?"

"Yes."

"Does he have to become a citizen of the Unites States?"

"No. It is his choice."

"Who is paying for this?"

"The United States Government."

"Can I have a car?"

"Not right away. You have to learn English first."

"How long?"

"Ninety days at least. Then a car is possible."

"What about my wife? Can she drive?"

"Yes., if she learns English first."

"What about Meena, my daughter?"

"If she is 16 years old or more, yes. she can drive."

"Will I have money?"

"Enough to get started. After that it will be up to you."

"If I have trouble, how do I get help?"

The Sergeant Major gave Wasim a business card. "Here is my phone number. Call me, day or night. You can also get help from the imam at the mosque and from the people you will meet at the mosque."

"Can I return with my family to Afghanistan if I want?"

"Yes."

"Will you give me money to return to Afghanistan?"

"Yes. We will put that in writing. You will get the farm in the United States, a car or truck, and money, if you agree in writing to never try to overthrow the government of the United States."

The Sergeant Major did not mention the CIA at this s point. They were providing the funding.

"Why are you doing this?"

"We do this because we want to get Borst. You and your family are eligible to immigrate into the United States because of persecution to you, the theft of your property, and sexual harassment of your family. You are eligible to come into the United States in accordance with our immigration laws. We believe that Abdul can help us do this, and he won't help us if it leaves you here with a dangerous future."

Wasim turned to Abdul.

"Abdul, do you want to do this?"

Abdul thought about it before he spoke. "I won't do it until I see you on the farm he talks about, with food and money. Then. Only then will I decide."

Abdul looked at Wasim.

"Sir, I want to marry your daughter."

Wasim nodded.

"Meena, will you marry me?"

"Yes."

Wasim looked directly at Sergeant Major Johnson.

"Why do you work for the government of the United States? You are black. Your people have had a terrible past in the United States. Don't you still have a bad time in your country because of your color?"

"Yes. We have a bad past. We have a past of slavery. They split up families. They sold people like me. They beat us and justified it to themselves. Then President Lincoln freed the slaves. The Constitution of the United States gave us our freedom. The Constitution of the United States gave us a vote. The Constitution is the law of the land. Some of the white people still tried to keep us from voting. Over time there have been some improvements. We are free. We vote. We hold important positions."

"What about in the Marine Corps? Are you treated the same as a white man?"

The Sergeant Major continued his explanation, "There are some bad people in the Marine Corps. But most people give us a fair chance. In the Declaration of Independence Thomas Jefferson wrote 'all men are created equal.' At the time, Thomas Jefferson was a man who owned slaves. He probably meant that all white men are created equal. Today, we consider that all men and all women are created equal and should be treated the same under the law. The Declaration of Independence was signed on July 4, 1776. That is America's birthday. That is more than 200 years ago. The men who signed that document would have been hung by the British King if they had lost their fight for independence. Sometimes you have to fight for what you think is right."

The Sergeant Major addressed Wasim. "Sir, talk it over with your family and with Abdul. Abdul, think about it. Let me know what you want to do."

There wasn't any dissent in the family. They knew that if they stayed on the farm they would be attacked again, killed, raped, or robbed. At least if they left, there would be a chance to live in peace, albeit in a foreign land.

"We will do it," Wasim told Sergeant Major Johnson. We will move to the United States. But we don't have passports, and we need to sell the farm."

Wasim knew that his cousin paid protection money to the Taliban. Wasim would sell his farm to his cousin.

Sergeant Major Johnson said, "I will take you to Kabul. It will be easier and faster to get passports there. He did not mention that there were agency assets there who would speed up the process.

The passports were expedited, and travel arrangements made to move Abdul, Wasim, and his family to the United States.

Following the Soviet invasion of Afghanistan in 1979, about five million Afghanis were displaced. Many found temporary asylum in neighboring Pakistan or Iran. Eventually many moved into Europe, North America, Oceana, and other places. By 1980 families moved into the United States. The largest population of Afghan Americans were in Fremont, California in the San Francisco Bay Area, Northern Virginia, and in Queens, in New York City. Wasim and his wife wanted to live on a farm. It was two weeks before they discovered that there was a farmer in Iowa who needed labor and had an empty house on his property.

"You can farm in Iowa?" Wasim asked.

"It is said that one quarter of the good topsoil of the United States is in Iowa."

This pleased Wasim. Within the next few years, he would find that it was so.

The Marine Corps let the Sergeant Major finish his tour in Afghanistan. His next assignment was to the Pentagon.

The Pentagon

Sergeant Major James Johnson, United States Marine Corps, sat at his desk in the Pentagon and checked his calendar for the day. A meeting was scheduled for 1600 (4:00 PM) in a SCIF, a Sensitive Compartmented Information Facility. It was the most classified conference room they had, and every branch of the service would be at this meeting.

The Sergeant Major began talking to himself, "Another meeting! Great! By the time this meeting is over the traffic will be terrible. If I get 20 bucks for every meeting I have to go to while I'm based in this stupid puzzle palace, I could retire a rich man." In fact, his Pentagon tour had just begun. He didn't like it.

By 1600 (4:00 PM) he had finished off a Power Bar and a cup of coffee. He grabbed his notebook and proceeded to the conference room. He was surprised to see a three-star general leading the meeting. Lieutenant General Tuttle, United States Army, addressed the group.

"Leave your cell phones outside gentlemen." The practice was SOP for a SCIF. "Also, leave your papers and notebooks outside. There will be no notetaking in this meeting."

After a few moments people found a place to sit and the room was quiet.

"We have had a problem with operational security gentlemen. Every time we have tried to take out this target, we have been thwarted. We have had good intel on his location more than once. We sent teams out to get him. We sent Rangers. No luck. We sent Green Berets. No luck. We sent Navy SEALS. No luck. He's not there. By the time the team is in position, he has vanished. We worked with the CIA and paid people in the region for information - to no avail. This target is an extremely bad actor. He conducted an operation that nearly destroyed a whole Army unit. He took out a SEAL team that we sent after him by shooting down their helicopter."

"So, this is what we came up with. We are going to put teams of two men each in the area to find him. These are two-man teams. It may be possible to include a native as one of the team members. One of the people will be an American, with a spec ops background. All candidates must be good at high elevation work, since that's where this work will be. These teams are going into Afghanistan in the area where the whole country is standing on its side, vertical, and higher up than any of you have ever been without an airplane. It would be nice if one of the teams could join the bad guy's group, under cover. We never tried that before. Obviously, one of the men has to speak Dari very well and be believable."

"We are going to do some training at high altitude. It's going to be winter. We know that. What we need right now is a plan of where to train and who will be candidates. That's where you come in. You pick the place and the people we are going to work with. Figure out right now who is going to come up with people, who is going to pick the location, who is going to supply it, who is going to train it, the whole nine yards. Start now. Report back to me tomorrow at 1600, right here."

Everyone walked out of the room except the General and an Army lieutenant.

"Well General, there is bad news and there is bad news."

This was ops normal for the military, so the General wasn't upset. "Why don't you give me the bad news first?"

"First, we have lost intel on our target in Afghanistan. Nobody, and I mean nobody, including none of our three letter friends, can find him. Second, Afghanistan's high mountains are supposed to really get clobbered with snow this winter. We didn't expect to have to train our guys for such cold weather conditions."

"What do you recommend?"

The Lieutenant looked at the General like a deer in the headlights.

"Well?"

No response.

"OK, Lieutenant, let this be a learning experience for you. We have a problem here, which means you have a problem here. You have two ways to approach this. You can walk up to your boss at his desk with your problem, dump the problem on his desk like a big hairy ball of shit, and say 'Ugh! There it is General. Now what?' Or you can say 'General, we have a problem. Describe the problem. Tell the boss what the essence of the problem is and describe options to tackle the problem. Like plan A, plan B, and plan C. I recommend plan A for this reason. So, Lieutenant, what do you recommend?"

"I would recommend we send the team to the Army Mountain Warfare School in Vermont. They specialize in cold weather and mountain ops. My problem is that they require a summer and winter training set, right?"

"Negative. TRADOC approved single phase qualification for the BMMC in 2008."

The Lieutenant was afraid to ask if BMMC stands for the Basic Military Mountaineer Course. He already felt stupid and didn't want to go downhill from there.

"Yes sir. I'll notify the school that we need 12 quotas, and I'll cut the orders as soon as we have names for the teams."

Before the meeting started, Sergeant Major Johnson had notified his fellow commuters in his carpool that he would not be with them tonight. That meant a late ride on the Metro. The Sergeant Major walked out of the meeting late when it was already dark outside.

Why had all attempts to get to this tough guy failed? What was lacking? Was it the training? The people? Their approach?

The Sergeant Major talked to himself, "Let's think about the training first. This is a mountain op, because every time we get close to the bad guy he disappears in the mountains. The Army has a good mountaineering school in Vermont." He looked at it on the internet:

Army Mountain Warfare School (AMWS) Jericho,

Vermont, Camp Ethan Allen Training Site (CEATS) "The gods of the hills are not the gods of the valleys" – Ethan Allen

The mountaineering school had classes starting in January and February, including:

1. Basic Military Mountaineer
2. Advanced Military Mountaineer
3. Mountain Rifleman's Course

He asked himself, "What if the elevations and the conditions are more extreme than they expect? What if they get separated from their gear?" The team needed a high elevation training site to be used in the dead of winter. He looked at a base the Army and Marines use in Hawaii.

The Pohkuloa Training Area is located on the Island of Hawaii, in the high plateau between Mauna Loa, Mauna Kea and the Hualalai volcanic mountains. The name of the current facility comes from *pu'u pōhaku loa*, which means "long rocky cinder cone" in the Hawaiian Language. It is used by both the U.S. Army and Marine Corps. The only road access is via the narrow Saddle Road (Hawaii Route 200), which is paralleled by a tank trail. Heavy equipment is either flown into Hilo, or else shipped via barge to Kawaihae Harbor, about 40 miles (64 km) away on the Saddle Road. Because of this remoteness, the area is used mostly for short training sessions.

The internet did not tell the story he wanted. From the camp they could also hike up Mauna Kea, 13,803 feet. That would provide a place where they could figure out who can handle some serious elevation. The first part of the problem is to get the intel. The second part is to find a high elevation place to train. The third part is to select people who can do this. What if this team has to work inside a town for a while, and has to buy food? What if they have to ask questions without raising red flags that give them away? The General said one of the guys of the two-man teams could be a local. A local would be good. If the team is comprised of only locals, could I trust them? It would be better if we make each team with one local guy and one American spec ops guy. One local guy to buy food and ask questions, and one American to keep the op on target and keep in contact with the leadership.

The approach to the problem was something he was going to have to think about. The people for the op... Where is that speed freak who ran around the whole base in basic training to reach Freedom Village in the search and evasion course? And what languages will they need? He had learned Dari when he was in the country. He had really worked at it. To confirm what he already knew, he checked the internet for Afghanistan's languages: "The official languages of the country are Dari and Pashto as established by the 1964 Constitution of Afghanistan. Dari is the most widely spoken language of Afghanistan's official languages, and acts as a lingua franca for the country. "The Sergeant Major liked to work with Marine Corporal Rogers, who was the guy who had recognized that Abdul had marked out the distances to all points on the road that led to Wasim's farmhouse in Afghanistan. Rogers was a person who thought outside the box, and this is a situation where that could be helpful. Corporal Rogers was now a newly promoted Sergeant, USMC.

The Sergeant Major got Sergeant Rogers to come to his office in the Pentagon. When Sergeant Rogers arrived at the office, the Sergeant Major explained that what they were going to discuss was strictly on a need to know, strictly off record. "You talk about this, and people could get killed. Got that?" Rogers acknowledged the need for secrecy. The Sergeant Major explained that they would operate in Afghanistan and may need to buy food or collect intel from the locals. Right away Rogers said, "What you need is women."

"Women? What?" The Sergeant Major was perplexed.

"Yes. Women. Number one, they are natural intel collectors. You ever watch women at parties? By the time they leave they know everything. Who is cheating on who? Whose kid got into college? All the men talk about is sports and like that."

"Number two, the women won't be seen as a threat in Afghanistan. They could buy food or ask questions without raising suspicions, especially if they are native speakers."

"Let the women operate in a city where there are lots of people. They can't go to some small village where everyone knows everyone. It has to be a city. Have them buy food at the local markets. Let them become familiar to the local people. If this op is funded well enough, they could buy food at more than one place, search out a larger information base."

"Are we looking for Borst? The guy who stole the farmer's crop one year and came back to do the same thing the next year?"

The Sergeant Major nodded, and Sergeant Rogers continued speaking, "We are looking for Borst, but he is so paranoid it may be easier to find his lieutenant or one of his soldiers. Borst may take precautions to protect himself that his soldiers don't do. So, we can look for his soldiers. What do soldiers want? Food or a flophouse. Have the women work on the places that sell food. The flophouse?"

The Sergeamt Major replied, "I hear you when it comes to food. OK. Thanks, Rogers. Talk to you later."

The next meeting for the Sergeant Major convened on time at 1600 the next afternoon. The three-star kicked it off and turned the meeting over to his Lieutenant, who already had a dozen Army nominees for the job, as well as some native language speakers. The Lieutenant said the candidates for the op should go through the three courses at Army Mountain Warfare School in Vermont: The Basic Military Mountaineer, the Advanced Military Mountaineer, and the Mountain Rifleman course.

The three-star asked, "Why not turn this into a competition and invite the other branches to participate? Also, I would like to know if anybody has any suggestions. Anybody?

Nobody spoke up, so the Sergeant Major Johnson offered a suggestion.

"It may be a good idea to get a fresh approach to this thing. We have tried it all the normal ways."

"Fresh approach?"

"Why don't we get some women in on this?"

"Oh, so you are trying to think out of the box?" was said by some wise guy in the room.

The comment was meant to be a joke, but nobody laughed, so the guy pressed his point.

"How would a woman be able to do something that a spec ops guy can't?"

The Sergeant Major suggested, "Can you picture a woman, dressed in traditional clothes, walking up to our bad guy, pulling a concealed pistol out of her burka, and shooting him? Or picture this: You have been to parties before. The men talk about the NFL and pound down a few beers, but by the time the women leave they know everything about everyone there. Who is dating who, who is cheating on who, whose kids are doing what. Remember when people were hunter-gatherers? The men did the hunting, and the women gathered the fruits. They also gather information."

"What else?" the General asked.

"Also, a woman, dressed in the local garb, speaking the local language, buying fruit at a local store, isn't likely to arouse suspicion like some burly guy would. She might be able to casually ask a question here and there."

"I like it," the three-star said. "Let's do it. Anything else?"

"Yes, sir. Let's make the competition include some high-altitude work. You know that Mauna Kea on Hawaii is 13,800 feet high? The Army and Marines already use the base that is there."

The General said, "OK, let's do it like this: Army, Navy, and Marines provide names from your service and an alternate person's name for each of your guys. We'll get the Air Force to provide some helo pilots. Lieutenant, do you have quotas for 12 guys at the mountain warfare school? Let's make that for 24 people. Anybody who has been through the school gets to go again for a refresher, plus we can evaluate them while they are there. Let's send all of them through the Army's Mountain school, then let's send them out to the Hawaii high altitude camp right after that for high altitude competition. For people, it means 12 Americans and 12 native speakers. Six candidates will be army guys, six guys will be either Marines or SEALS. The CIA gets us the 12 native speakers. Four of the candidates will be women. Make that six women, including three native speakers and three Americans. You guys figure it out. Plus have one alternate for each primary. So that means the Army has six primaries and six alternates. Navy and Marines, same. Let's meet here at 1600 tomorrow with names. I'll get the CIA to provide the native speakers. They can go to the mountain warfare school too, and work right alongside the spec ops guys when we get to that phase of the op."

Among the U.S. Army personnel selected for the op was Staff Sergeant (E-6) Kristen Kraska. She qualified as expert on rifle and pistol, and was jump qualified. What set her apart was that she was member of a national championship cross country team while in college. She was officially contacted and volunteered for the assignment.

When Kristen learned that she would be teamed up with an Afghani woman and expected to climb mountains as part of a two-person team, she asked to be teamed up with the most athletic woman they could find. Kristen also asked that this woman be directed to get to the Army Mountain Warfare School immediately to start running and lifting weights with her. The CIA found a woman soccer player who grew up in Afghanistan until she was thirteen years old, when her family moved to Queens, New York. She resumed playing soccer when she got to the United States. She had quit playing soccer in Afghanistan about the time she hit puberty. She completed high school in the United States and spoke good English. Her name was Kaamisha.

The Agency provided a female escort for Kaamisha and a driver for the six-hour drive from New York City to The Army Mountain Warfare School in Vermont. She arrived there a bit tired from the trip but ready to start training. Kristen met her upon her arrival.

"Did you bring your workout gear?"

"Sure. I brought lots."

"Good. I'll show you your room. Get into your gear. We can go to the gym."

At the gym Kristen and Kaamisha did some stretches, walked on the treadmills for ten minutes, then did some slow jogging for a mile.

"Kaamisha, now that we are warmed up, show me how you run."

After three minutes on the treadmill running at a good clip, Kristen said, "That's good. You can stop. Let's work on your form."

"They told me you were a runner," Kaamisha said.

"Yes. I did a lot of running. With coaches. Running is about good form. Don't waste energy. Make sure your arms move straight forward and straight back. Too many women move their arms side to side, and waste energy. I'll show you."

Kristen jogged so that her hands were raised up as high as her chin with each stroke. Her hands weren't low, like untrained athletes do it.

"Practice that. Arms up. Hands moving straight forward and back. Yes. That's good."

"Now, your head should be up. Look ten meters ahead."

"Don't drag your feet. Your right heel is dragging. Pick up your feet. If you drag your feet, you slow yourself down. If your foot drags, it acts like a brake." They practiced the form together.

"One more thing. If you want to go faster, lean forward. Your body should be straight from your heel to your neck. That's why you look 10 meters ahead. And don't try to land on the balls of your feet. That's for sprinters. If you try to do that for long-distance running, you could injure yourself."

Kristen thought about mentioning the importance of pushing with the ankles but decided to hold that instruction until later.

"I'll show you some movies when we get back to our quarters. First let's get some food."

They jogged back to their quarters, showered, and got ready for dinner.

"I feel intimidated by you. You are so fast," Kaamisha said.

"I should feel intimidated by you. You speak Dari."

"You don't? Not Dari? What about Pashto?"

"No."

"Arabic?"

"No."

"Urdu?"

"No."

Kaamisha groaned. "Oh God. We are going to go into Afghanistan. I know it. That's why they wanted me. And I will never keep up with you in the mountains, and you don't speak a word of the language. We are going to be like that TV show."

"What TV show?"

"The Odd Couple."

Sergeant Major Johnson had several names in mind as candidates for this op, both American and Afghani. The people that he had the highest hope for were Ronnie

Stepovich and Abdul. I could team them up, he was thinking. After a couple of phone calls Johnson learned that Stepovich was on R and R, rest and recuperation leave, at his home. He telephoned the Stepovich residence.

"Is this Ronnie? Ronnie Stepovich? Hey Marine! How's it going? This is Sergeant Major Johnson calling from the Pentagon."

"Is this the same Sergeant Major Johnson from boot camp?"

"You remembered me? Good for you. Say, how's it going? I heard you took a hit and spent some time in hospital."

"Yeah, I did, but I'm doing fine. What can I do for you?"

"Well, I'm trying to put together a team to do some good stuff and I thought maybe you would be interested. The thing is, it will take some mountain training and it may be strenuous. How are you feeling?"

"I'm feeling pretty good. When would this be?"

"I think you can count on finishing the holidays at home, but you would have to be ready for the assignment by about mid-January. You think you could handle that?"

"I don't see why not. What kind of work is it?"

"We won't get into that on the phone. Can you pass a PFT?" He used the term for a Physical Fitness Test.

"No problem."

"OK Marine. Be prepared to take a PFT when you come back to work. I'll get the dates and locations to you as soon as I have them. Give me your cell phone number and email address too. I'll give you mine too. You can call me anytime, day or night. OK, ready to copy?"

Stepovich copied the phone numbers then hung up the phone. Mountain training school? This is going to be fun.

Chapter 7

Army Mountain Warfare School, Vermont

Ronnie Stepovich met Sergeant Major Johnson and Lieutenant Gilmere at the Mountain Warfare School in Vermont.

"Ronnie," the Sergeant Major explained, "Some admin types in the Corps think you have broken service because they thought you were dead. They closed out your service record, so they want you to reenlist to keep your record straight. If you do reenlist, you will be advanced to sergeant today. Are you willing to do that?"

"Yes."

"Good. The oath must be administered by a commissioned officer. Please stand in front of Lieutenant Gilmere," the Sergeant Major said.

Lieutenant Gilmere said, "Raise your right hand and repeat after me."

"I, Ronald Stepovich, do solemnly swear that I will support and defend the Constitution of the United States against all enemies foreign and domestic; that I will bear true faith and allegiance to the same; and that I will obey the orders of the President of the United States and the orders of the officers appointed over me, according to regulations, and the Uniform Code of Military Justice. So help me God."

"Congratulations, Sergeant Stepovich," the Sergeant Major said. This is an Army base, and they may not have the correct uniforms for you. However, the Lieutenant and I happen to have a set of chevrons for a sergeant, United States Marine Corps, along with a couple of shirts that should fit you with sergeant's chevrons. Congratulations, Marine!"

"Thank you, Sergeant Major. Thank you, Lieutenant."

While Ronnie was busy with the Lieutenant and the Sergeant Major in a back room in the building, the rest of the recruits for the special op were assembled at the mountaineering school in Vermont in January, in the dead of winter. They sat on benches in a small room and were told to await the commanding officer of the school. They had a few minutes to kill because they had arrived early.

"It's colder than hell here," somebody blurted out.

"How can hell be cold?" one candidate retorted.

"It's cold all right. This place has a reputation of being hell in the winter, and it's colder than hell."

"Hell is supposed to be hot. It can't be hot in this place."

Stinko entered the room at that point and sat on one of the benches. He noticed a plaque on the wall in the back of the room. It read:

Murphy's Law

1. Nothing is as easy as it looks.
2. Everything takes longer than you think.
3. If it can go wrong, it will, usually at the worst possible moment.

"I can see this place is going to be really swell," he surmised.

Sergeant Major James Johnson, United States Marine Corps, walked into the back of the room. He had been among the few senior enlisted people, military officers, and CIA special agents who had selected the recruits for this operation. Those recruits were candidates, really. They now sat in the small room in the cold, in Vermont, in the winter.

Sergeant Major Johnson walked to the front of the room and addressed the group.

"The commanding officer will join us shortly and kick this thing off. In the meantime, let's go around the room and introduce ourselves. Stand up, give us the name you want to go by while you are in training. I don't care about your rank, and I don't care where you came from. Your rank is student, and your rank will continue to be student until you are told otherwise. Anybody who tries to use his rank while he or she is in training will be expelled immediately. Got that? You people came from many branches of the service and from several countries. Your job will be to work together and learn together."

The Sergeant Major repeated what he had just said in Dari, for the benefit of the Afghani recruits. He then said in English, "We will start up here in the front row and work toward the back. Stand up, face the group, and say what name you want to go by. One name is enough, not a full name."

A few people introduced themselves before Stinko took his turn.

"My name is Stinko." That got a few laughs.

He sat down and listened as the others introduced themselves. When Abdul stood up to introduce himself, the Sergeant Major was amazed to see Stinko take a running leap, clear two rows of benches, land on top of Abdul, and start punching him. Stinko landed one punch when Abdul got his foot into Stinko's chest and shoved him so hard that Stinko went flying over the bench behind him, landing with his spine on the bench. The Sergeant Major and a couple of other recruits grabbed the two brawlers and kept them apart.

"You two idiots come with me!" the Sergeant Major shouted. "The rest of you wait here and don't talk!"

The Sergeant Major led them into an office in the back. "Sit down, you two! You want to get thrown out of the Corps, Stepovich?"

Ronnie was silent.

"You want to get thrown out of this program before it even starts, Abdul?" The question was repeated in Dari.

"You two cool off and get it together."

Abdul didn't understand everything that was said, but he understood when it was time to shut up.

"Explain yourself Stepovich."

"This is the guy who shot me. We had his picture in Fallujah and were looking for him."

"Let's take this one step at a time," the Sergeant Major

suggested. "Are you two calm enough to listen for a change?" He repeated what he asked in Dari.

Nobody said a word, so he continued.

"Stepovich, let's start with you. Why are you here? Start at the beginning."

"You know why I'm here, Sergeant Major. You recruited me from boot camp for force recon, and you selected me for this op, whatever it is."

"No, I don't know why you are here. Why are you in the Marine Corps?"

The Sergeant Major translated each of his replies into Dari.

"I joined after 9/11," Stinko said.

"Why? Why did you join?"

"A friend of mine and I decided it was the right thing to do."

"What were you doing before you joined?"

"I was at Northern Illinois University, on a baseball team. My friend Jack Russell and I decided to drop out of school and join up."

"Was it you who convinced your friend?"

"No. It was more like the other way around."

"Why did you listen to this guy Jack?"

"Jack was my best friend. Still is."

"How did you meet this best friend?"

"I was a loner as a kid. Nobody played with me. Then Jack started coming to my house every day and took me out to play baseball, every day in the summer. Pretty soon we became friends. After that we sort of found out that I could run and hit pretty good, and I started hanging out with other guys. Jack got me out of my shell, sort of."

"So, you went to boot camp. Tell me about what you did when you had to sneak through a couple of miles of terrain, not get caught, not get seen, and make it to the Freedom Village."

"Yeah, well, my partner and I figured we would make like a snake and crawl in the mud every chance we got. So, we came out of that covered in mud and smelling like a swamp, but we made it."

"Did anyone else make it?"

"No, we were the only ones."

"Then your company, meaning all the trainees in boot camp, did poorly on that operation so they had to do it again, right?"

"Yeah."

"OK, genius, tell us what happened."

"Well, all the instructors knew we made it the day before by crawling through the swamp. We knew they would watch that swamp carefully, so we decided to do something different."

"Yes?"

"We backtracked, went directly away from the Freedom Village for about a half of a mile, then went out to the perimeter road that ran around the base. We ran the perimeter road for a few miles, then climbed over the fence and got to the Freedom Village from the back side, where they didn't expect us to be."

"OK, then what?"

"Then, you were the Sergeant Major in charge of training, and you suggested that I might like force recon. So, I applied and got in."

The Sergeant Major knew Ronnie's record. To earn the designation as a Reconnaissance Marine, MOS 0321, Ronnie had to satisfactorily complete the Advanced Infantry Battalion (AITB) of the School of Infantry (West), Marine Corps Base Camp Pendleton, California. The Special Operations Training Group (SOTG) bases include, among others, Camp Pendleton California, and Camp Smedley D. Butler, Okinawa Prefecture, Japan, named for the Marine who was twice awarded the Congressional Medal of Honor.

After he had proved himself in an operational environment, he had further trained with the SOTG. There he completed the Assault Climbers Course, five weeks, three phases: the Helicopter Rope Suspension Techniques (HRST) Masters Course, and the Deep Infiltration and Extraction Team (DIFT) Course. Repeating all this formal training would not inform Abdul what the Sergeant Major wanted him to know.

"Did you do OK in force recon?"

"I guess. I'm here anyway."

Abdul understood a bit of what Ronnie had been saying. The Sergeant Major had translated the rest. Abdul remembered Stepovich from Fallujah. Abdul had seen him there and had seen him run up and down the street, pulling injured men out of the street, and taking cover using buildings, cars, and trucks. Abdul had mentally given Stepovich the nickname "cheetah" because he was the fastest runner he had ever seen.

"What is your friend Jack doing now?"

"He's a pilot in the Marine Corps."

"OK, Stepovich, thank you. Do you think you can just sit and listen for a moment?"

"Yes, sir."

"Abdul, why are you here?"

"You know."

"Yes. Please explain it to me. Speak Dari if you want. I'll translate, one sentence at a time."

"I was living on a farm in Afghanistan with Wasim and my fiancée. We were raising wheat. The Taliban came and stole all the wheat from Wasim the year before I got there. So, Wasim and I went to town and bought some guns. Some pistols and rifles. When the Taliban came the next time, we stopped them."

"How many Taliban were there?"

"Ten."

"How did you know what they wanted?"

"They all had guns and came driving up the road in trucks. They were armed like that, with rifles, when they had stolen his wheat before."

"So, what did you do?"

"I shot the tires on the first truck."

"What did they do?"

"They started shooting at me from the trucks. With rifles."

"Then what did you do?"

"I started shooting drivers."

"Did you have a range finder?"

"No."

"How far away were they when you started shooting?"

Eight hundred meters."

"How did you know the distance?"

"I had put big rocks along the road and painted them red and white, so I knew how far away they were."

"So, you killed ten Taliban."

"No."

"No? I don't understand."

"Meena killed two men, in the house. They were trying to rape her."

"Did she have a rifle?"

"Pistol."

"How did she get the pistol?"

"I told you. Wasim and I bought them in town."

"How did she know how to use a pistol?"

"I taught her."

"Why?"

"Because there are men like this in the Taliban. They think a woman is to be used."

"Meena is?"

"My fiancée."

"How long were you on the farm?"

"A year."

"How did you get there?"

Abdul was silent.

"How did you get to the farm? Why were you at the farm?"

Abdul didn't answer. It was silent for a minute.

The Sergeant Major guessed the reason for the silence.

"Did you fight the Americans before? We know you did. You shot Stepovich in Fallujah. That was before. Tell us what changed."

The Sergeant Major thought it would help if he told them something about his own past. He looked at Abdul and said, "Let me explain something. I am in the Marine Corps today, but my past is not pretty. I got into the Marine Corps because a judge told me that I could either join the military or go to jail. I joined the Marine Corps. Today I want to live the way of truth. I realize that may sound weird, but it is what I want to do at this point of my life. That helps me to live with my family, to work with my fellow Marines, and to feel peace spiritually."

He spoke slowly. He repeated some of it in English.

The Sergeant Major looked at Abdul calmly. "You can live the way of truth, Abdul. Why were you on the farm?"

Abdul didn't know why he trusted the Sergeant Major. The man wasn't from his part of the world. The man didn't practice the same religion that he did. The man wasn't from his ethnic group. He was black. A black American. Abdul sat for a minute.

"I didn't want to fight Americans. I had no choice."

"No choice?" The Sergeant Major nodded his head. His face was calm.

"I had no choice," Abdul repeated. I was raised in Iraq. Abdul did not say Baghdad. My father beat me from the time I was small. When I got big enough to fight back, he didn't beat me so often. He started beating my mother. He did it again and again. I asked him to stop. I told him to stop. One time he beat her again, badly. Then he beat me with a wrench. I hit him on the head with a brick. He died. I dumped his body in the river in the middle of the night."

"I felt bad. Not about my father, but about my mother. Who would provide for her? I was afraid. I didn't know what the police would do if they found out. I talked to the imam at our mosque. He said I could be forgiven the sin if I agreed to serve Allah by joining the Mujahedeen in Afghanistan."

"Did you know how to be a soldier?"

"No."

"Did you know how to shoot?"

"No."

"How did you learn?"

"They teach me."

"Teach you what?"

"How to hike. How to camp. How to cook. How to hide in the mountains. How to take care of rifle."

"How to shoot?"

"That came later."

"How did they do that?"

"We had to learn the parts of the rifle. We had to clean it."

"What kind of rifle"

"AK47."

"Did you shoot right away?"

"No. First it was just learn the parts of the rifle. Take it apart. Clean it. Again, and again. Later it was sighting."

"Why?"

"Save bullets. We had few."

"Then what?"

"All of us shoot. Just a few of us they pick for more training."

"Training as what?"

"Sniper."

"Did many people train?"

"No. Only a few. Later they got snipers together."

"For what?"

"More training."

"Were you good at it?"

Abdul didn't answer.

"Abdul, were you good at it?"

"Uh,"

"Was there a competition?"

"Yes. Many."

"And?"

No reply.

"Abdul, what happened?"

"The lead instructor said I was the best he ever saw."

"Did you work as a sniper?"

"Yes."

"How long?"

"For years."

"How many years?"

"Five years before the Americans came."

"Were you in the mountains or in a city?"

"Both. Mostly in the mountains."

"Were you ever high up in the mountains?"

"Yes."

"Many times?"

"Yes."

"OK, you two. We have a hard operation coming up. We need people who can do the job. We are going to put together teams of two men, one who speaks Dari, and one who is an American who is strong enough to function in the mountains. That is why you are here in this mountain school. I'm not going to tell you any more at this point, except that I want you two to be a team."

"Here we go," Stinko said to himself.

"Am I supposed to work with this freak?" Abdul asked himself.

"Abdul, you need to get accepted by the people in this group. You will have to work with them, day by day. You need a new name. Your real name is Abdul, so how about something like…"

"Ali?" he suggested.

"Ali? That's the son-in-law of the prophet Muhammad. That might not be right for this group."

"His name is Abdul, so let's call him 'Dool' like in 'Drool,' Stinko was thinking.

"How about…"

"Al?"

"Al is good. You have to pronounce 'Al' like 'pal.' The 'A' has to sound like the 'A' in 'Hat' or the 'A' in 'Cat,' the Sergeant Major replied.

How about the 'A' in 'Rat' Stinko was thinking. Or the 'A' in 'Ass?'

The Sergeant Major said, "Say 'Al,' and make the 'A' sound like the 'A' in 'Hat.'

Abdul couldn't master the pronunciation.

"I got a better idea," the Sergeant Major said. Your name is Hot Shot."

They were ready to join the group.

After they rejoined the group, someone shouted, "Attention on Deck!" Everyone stood at attention as the commanding officer of AMWS, Army Mountain Warfare School, marched to the front of the room.

"Seats!"

"Ladies and gentlemen, this is the Army Mountain Warfare School. HIGHER!"

"We adjusted our schedule considerably to get you into each of the three courses we teach here. If you finish the Basic Military Mountaineer Course successfully you will get your Ram's Head Insignia, then proceed to the Advanced Military Mountaineer Course. If you finish that successfully you will proceed to the Mountain Rifleman's Course."

"You will learn things here that you never learned before, even if you have been here before. We have incorporated lessons learned from Afghanistan."

"I am not going to take up any more of your time, except to tell you one thing. This is winter and it is cold. Real cold. Your experience here is going to suck. But that doesn't mean that you go off and make some emotional decision. An emotional decision is like quitting. Do not, and I say again, DO NOT think about what you are doing this afternoon. Do not think about tomorrow, or next week. Make it through the session you are in. That's it. Just concentrate on the lesson you are doing, finish it, and you will make it."

"Attention on deck!"

Everyone stood up and the commanding officer left.

The Sergeant Major walked to the front of the room.

"This is a military school. United States Army, in fact. But we are not funded by the military. This operation is funded by the CIA. This is the last time you will hear those letters, so you can forget about it. You will not read about this operation in your service records."

"In a military course you still have rank. We are going to run this a little differently. We are going to go by first names. Nobody gets to pull rank here. There is a reason for this. You are going to operate in teams. You are going to need to use your brain to stay alive. You are going to have to use ideas to succeed. Each person needs to think. Each person needs to share ideas. We tried to do the introductions a few minutes ago and a fight broke out before we finished. So, we are going to start over again and do it until we finish. We are going to go around the room and introduce ourselves to each other. Just one name. Don't tell me where you came from. Just one name. He pointed to a guy in the front row. You start."

When Abdul stood up, the Sergeant Major spoke up for him. "This man is called Hot Shot. You will call him Hot Shot."

There were two teams that had women. The first woman who stood up said, "My name is Kristen."

Her partner stood up and said, "I am Kaamisha." The two of them got to be known as the KK Team.

There was a redneck named Bern sitting in the back of the room. "Why are there women in this class?" he blurted out.

"If we wanted you to know that we would tell you, moron!" the Sergeant Major shouted. "Now sit down, shut up, and listen!"

There were a lot of teams with people who looked fit enough. There was a team that had an Army Ranger named Gomez who teamed up with a guy from Afghanistan named Gujar. They became known as the GG Team.

When the introductions were done, the Sergeant Major said, "I am an instructor here. Instructors have rank. My name is Sergeant Major. When you get to know me well you can call me Sergeant Major."

During the first week of Army Mountaineering School, Abdul observed that Stepovich overestimated his own abilities. Stinko tried to climb up a vertical wall using his fingers to jam into a crack, left hand pulling left, right hand pulling right, and jamming his toes into the crack any way he could. Stinko lost contact with the rock face at 80 feet from the ground and would have fallen to his death had it not been for a belay rope, a safety line, which held his fall because Abdul was firmly anchored above him, controlling his belay line. Abdul saved him. It would not be the last time. Ronnie made a habit of going up the hardest climb, in minimum time. Then he would fall. Happened every time.

Abdul observed that his partner underestimated the difficulty of the climb and overestimated his own ability. Stinko thought that because he could easily handle the beginner and intermediate climbs, he could tackle the hardest climbs. He was wrong. Stinko fell off the rock face repeatedly. Only the belay line held him. After each failure he tried it again. Same result. Due to his speed, Ronnie would lead the climbs. Due to his overconfidence and lack of respect for the mountain, he would get them killed.

It was cold, and it was hard, but they completed the courses. They finished the Basic Military Mountaineer Course and got their Ram's Head Insignia. They finished the Advanced Military Mountaineer Course. They finished the Mountain Rifleman's Course.

115

Jennifer's cell phone rang.

"Ronnie?"

"Jen, great news! I have a week off!"

"Cool! Are you coming home?"

"No. Can you meet me in Colorado?"

"Colorado? What's going on?"

"Can't get into that right now. Can you meet me at the Denver International Airport? I can get there by 9:30 PM Friday night, Mountain Standard Time. We can spend a whole week in Breckenridge. It is only an hour and a half from Denver. I can get a great room for the week. They are giving us a break before we start the next training session. We can book flights out of Denver on the following Saturday, or even Sunday, if you like. I'll buy some chains for the car in case there is snow."

"Sounds good to me. You said Sunday is possible. That gives us one more day. Let's do a Sunday departure. Should I pick up anything special? Ski clothes?" Jennifer asked.

"Bring some fitness gear and hiking boots. We can use the gym at the hotel or go to a fitness center."

"What else?"

"I'll rent a car and get the chains for the tires."

"OK. Is there anything I can do?"

"There is. This is a huge favor, but can you get an English teacher to come with us? My partner can come too, and I will be sure that the teacher and he have their own rooms, but I think he won't come if I can't plan something productive for him."

"I'll see what I can do. Why Breckenridge?"

"Its elevation is 9600 feet, and it is bound to have great restaurants. That's all I'm supposed to say. Let me know if we need a room for our English teacher."

Jen knew a lady who used to teach English as a Second Language. Jen asked her if she would be available for a week to teach classes for seven hours a day in Colorado. Her friend was retired and jumped at the opportunity. They agreed on a fair fee, including money for food, and Jen said she would pay for the flights and the room. Stinko would get the car and they would meet at the airport at the baggage claim for her flight.

Jen knew that Ronnie had been in the Army Mountain Warfare School, so his plan to vacation at high elevation had a certain logic to it. Besides, she could try skiing if it got boring.

The time in Breckenridge went fast. Abdul worked for seven hours a day with the English teacher. In the late afternoon, he and Stinko hiked together in the high elevation of the city. Every hiking session ended with some running.

They both were out of breath from the elevation and the exertion, but that didn't stop Abdul from asking a question.

"Hey, Stinko?"

"Yeah."

"Why should I put up with you?"

"Because I'm so smart and handsome?'

"You are not. You are a moron!"

"Listen to you! You've been learning new words lately! For a stupid raghead you talk like a real person!"

"Me? A stupid raghead? You are a stupid honky!"

"Camel jockey!"

"Wife beater!"

"Pussy whipped!"

They both smiled.

Chapter 8

Mauna Kea, Hawaii

Bern Jackson was from a small town in Arkansas. Bern liked his friends to be white, his politicians to be male, and his women to be docile. Bern's thinking went like this: "We been on this here mountain fer days and I kin see one dang thing fer certain. I know talent when I see it. Mrs. Jackson didn't raise no dummies. I just can't believe it's the freak and the foreigner who have all the talent."

Bern had watched Stinko and Abdul outperform everyone else back at the Army Mountain Warfare School. They all had completed the Mountain Rifleman's Course. It was obvious that Abdul could really shoot. Abdul was hands down the best shooter in the group. It wasn't even close. And that guy Stinko can really move.

Stinko watched Bern walk toward him. Stinko had observed Bern in the competition. He had also listened to Bern and decided that Bern was not the sort of person he wanted to hang out with.

"They call you Stinko, right?"

"My friends call me that. I didn't say you could call me that."

"OK, Stinko. You are some sort of Marine Recon expert, right? Why are you hanging around with this raghead?"

Stinko walked away without a reply.

An Army Ranger from one of the teams walked up to

Abdul and said, "Hot Shot, don't listen to that guy. I'm from the South, just like he is, and I have nothing but respect for what you do."

"Thanks," Abdul replied.

Sergeant Major Johnson, USMC, convened the 24 candidates in a trailer at the 10,000-foot level in the saddle between Mauna Kea and Mauna Loa, on the big island of Hawaii.

"The reason you are here, ladies and gentlemen, is to acclimate to high elevation and to demonstrate your shooting ability in the mountains. All hiking you do here will be timed. All shooting you do here will be recorded. It is a competition. When you hike up the mountain, you must hike as a team. Perhaps I should say climb up the mountain, for that is exactly what you will be doing. Your climbs will be timed. Your descents will be timed. You must, and I repeat must stay with your teammate. That means your time will be dictated by the rate that your slower teammate can handle. If you want to carry your teammate, you can. You won't want to do that. If you separate from your teammate, your team is disqualified. Are there any questions?"

"What rifle are we shooting?"

"Today it's an M4."

"Why not a sniper rifle?"

"You will get sniper rifles when you get used to climbing at this elevation. Your sniper rifle will weigh 14 pounds. Your M4A1 weighs 7.62 pounds with a sling and loaded magazine."

"7.62 is a caliber," Bern interjected.

"You are not telling me anything I don't already know, soldier."

"What about a ghillie suit?"

"The ghillie suit weighs 4.75 pounds to six pounds, depending on size. You don't have to carry that weight today because you have not fully acclimated to this elevation."

"We use this trailer as our dining room. When you finish supper tonight, here in this trailer, you will be given a pad of paper and a pencil. Write down all the gear you will need. Include sniper rifle, model of binoculars you prefer, NVGs (Night Vision Goggles), model of ghillie suit, whether you prefer to build your own ghillie suit, model of range detector, sunscreen, bug repellent preferences, thermal socks, knives, peanut butter, granola, anything. Print your name and sign it. I'll see what I can do. You don't have to have the same gear as the next guy."

"The list we give you tonight will already contain all the gear that I just mentioned plus first aid gear and thermal underwear. All you have to do is put down your preference, if you have one. If you don't have a preference, we will pick something for you."

"Do the women get a handicap?"

"No. Same standard for everyone."

"Any more questions? There should be one more question. You should ask, how will the teams be selected to go on the op? That will be decided by your performance here, based on three things:

1. Your hiking times.
2. Your shooting scores.
3. The assessment of the instructors whether you can work with us and with each other to achieve our goals.

"You mean our scores at the Army Mountain Warfare School don't count?"

"Of course, those scores count. You passed. It got you here. Any more questions?"

There were no more questions.

"There is water, fruit, granola, peanut butter, and some drinks on the truck outside the trailer. Pick some up. Be sure to pack a poncho, spare socks, and dry shirts in your backpack. Bring some spare TP and first aid for blisters. Use the heads that you see behind the trailer. We will start the timed evolution from outside this trailer in 15 minutes. Check your watches now. You have 15 minutes."

This morning the candidates had to complete a 3000-foot climb from an elevation of 10,000 feet above sea level to 13,000 feet above sea level. They knew that the climb was timed, and their performance was recorded. The mountain that they were on, Mauna Kea, rises to 13,803 feet, so they wouldn't reach the top.

They were allowed to climb on the cinder road that led from the saddle up to the observatory on the top of the mountain. The cinder road was packed, but the footing wasn't as good as it is on some surfaces. There was slippage.

They were about halfway up the mountain when

Kaamisha let Kristen know what she thought about the pace.

"Kristen, you are killing me!"

"You are doing great, Kaamisha. Keep it up," Kristen replied.

"What are we doing here? I speak Dari. Am I supposed to translate for a mountain goat? Nobody will want to talk to me at 13,000 feet. Anybody at this elevation will have a rifle in his hands and won't talk Dari or any other language. They will shoot first, talk later."

"Suck it up girl. We got to do this together."

"Yeah, yeah. Translate this, woman!" Kaamisha replied and let out a few choice words in Dari.

"I'm sure I don't want to know what you just said, translator lady!"

She got a smile out of Kaamisha on that comment.

Stinko and Abdul were the first ones to make it to the 13,000-foot level. The female team with Kristen and Kaamisha, the "KK Team," was the next team to make it.

Once everyone made it to the 13,000-foot level, the instructors told them that they had 20 minutes to set up a shooting position. Each person had to fire three shots at a target that was 500 meters from their makeshift shooting positions. They were firing the M4 rifle close to the limit of its effective range. The M16 would be slightly more accurate and would have minimally more range, but the M16 had a longer barrel, had more weight, and lacked the carrying handle that made the M4 easier to use.

The instructors recorded each person's score. Other instructors covered the holes in the targets with patches, so the targets could be reused. As usual, Abdul had the top score and Stinko was not far behind. Army Ranger Gomez and his partner Goja were the first team to get down to the 10,000-foot level, followed by Stinko and Abdul, then Kristen and Kaamisha.

Bern could see that his team was falling behind in the competition. Bern decided to try to get a better relationship going with Stinko and Abdul. He walked over to Stinko when Abdul was nearby.

"Hey Stepovich, maybe we uh, like got off on the wrong foot."

"That's all you got buddy, two wrong feet."

"Yeah, well maybe. My name is Bern. Bern Jackson."

"What's your other name? Everyone calls you Redneck."

"Yeah. I'm a redneck and proud of it. My other name is John. Bern John Jackson."

"You can call me Stinko. Everyone else does. I'm going to call you BJ."

"BJ? Why you damn Yankee! I ought to deck you!"

"You could try."

Bern chuckled. "Well, I see you got a sense of humor Where you all from?"

"Does it matter?"

"Not really. Hey, my teammate doesn't like the food they gave us. He said I could have it. I could share it with you."

Stinko never turned down food.

Bern walked away, and Abdul walked up to Stinko and said, "What does he want?"

"It looks like his partner is getting sick. You can see it. If his partner quits, that will leave old BJ without a partner. This idiot thinks he can beat me in the competition and team up with you, because you are winning all the shooting competitions."

"I don't want to work with him. He called me a raghead," Abdul replied.

"You can learn something from him. You can learn how a good ole Southern boy talks. Some day when we are doing one of our great operations in the high mountains, I might get shot, and you would have to talk on the radio to get us out of there. You might have to talk to someone with this big old accent to get us help. This is your big chance to master a new accent in the English language."

"Talk, like that?"

"It's a skill. Just think. You could be the first kid on your block to speak like a hick."

"A hick?"

"Yeah. A hick. A hick is like a jerk, an idiot, a dumb guy, from some place way out in the middle of nowhere. We call places like that the boondocks, or the sticks. People from there are hicks."

"Hicks from the sticks?"

"Yeah, you got it."

The training turned into a routine. Each day consisted of climbing up the mountain, practice at hiding in the cinders and rocks, shooting, and descending. Everything was done at a breakneck pace. Their lungs burned, their mouths were dry, their lips cracked, their legs ached, their ankles hurt, their calves cramped up.

The KK Team of Kristen and Kaamisha were able to outclimb everyone except Stinko and Abdul. One afternoon during a break Stinko asked the Sergeant Major who Kristen was.

"Her? She went to BYU and was on the cross-country team."

"BYU?" Stinko asked.

"Yes. Brigham Young University, in Utah. BYU won the NCAA cross country championship four times, and twice while she was on the team."

"It shows," Stinko replied.

When they did escape and evasion drills, they had to use what little cover the mountain provided. Mauna Kea is volcanic, and there is little in the way of terrain to hide behind. The best way to disappear in this terrain was to get into the low spots and lie still. Movement attracts attention.

Sometimes they were in the trailer studying maps of Afghanistan. Knowing the terrain can save your life. Knowledge is life. That's what the instructor said. Sometimes while Stinko studied terrain, Abdul worked with a language instructor, improving English skill. There were several language instructors in the camp.

During a lull in the training sergeant Major Johnson

asked Ronnie and Abdul to join him at a table in the back of one of the trailers. He asked Abdul the following questions:

"Abdul, do you think that the Taliban are as bad a threat to the United States as the Al Qaeda?"

"No. Al Qaeda worse."

"Why?"

"Al Qaeda want to attack the United States in the United States."

"The Taliban doesn't want to attack the United States?"

"Not in the United States. Taliban is tribes. They want to control their tribe and take care of family, in Afghanistan. Taliban not interested in attack in the United States."

The Sergeant Major asked another question. "The ISIL is the Islamic State of Iraq and the Levant. They were Al Qaeda before, right?"

Abdul nodded yes.

"And the Levant is the countries along the eastern Mediterranean, like modern day Israel, Jordan, Lebanon, and Syria, right? Some people include Egypt, part of east Libya, Turkey, and part of Greece, right?"

"Yes."

"But the ISIL does not include Jews from Israel?"

"No. Of course, not."

The Islamic State, known as ISIL, ISIS (Islamic State in Iraq and Syria), or Daesh in Arabic, would later declare itself a caliphate and take over large swaths of Iraq and Syria.

"Do the Taliban want a caliphate worldwide?"

"Not their goal. Taliban is tribal. Stay in Afghanistan."

"What about Al Qaeda?"

"Yes. Caliphate. Worldwide Islamic state."

"Bin Laden is Al Qaeda."

"Yes."

"Al-Zawahiri?"

"Yes."

"They want a jihad? And the jihadis are the warriors? The jihadi would kill all Jews and Christians. And Hindus. Any religion not Islamic, right?"

"Yes. Jihadis will kill anyone who will not use force to work for the jihad, even Muslims."

"They would kill other Muslims?"

"Yes. Jihadis must fight for the goal to have a caliphate, a worldwide Muslim state, or die."

After seven days on Mauna Kea on the "big island" of Hawaii, an instructor called the group together in a trailer at the 10,000-foot level. There were still 24 men and women in the group, divided into 12 teams. Each team was either all male or all female.

"OK, girls. Your training has been hiking, climbing, shooting, map reading, and terrain hugging. You know that. Exactly where you are going is not for general distribution yet, so I won't tell you. I won't tell you because I do not know, and I would not tell you even if I did know. It doesn't take a genius to figure out that you are going somewhere in the mountains, which is why you are up here in this lovely place."

"Another part of your training is survival. Survival

means just that. Surviving. Staying alive. I had hoped we could skip this part of the training, but somebody in the Pentagon decided that this is the way it is going to be. Here is the deal. The jet stream has taken a big bend and is now down south. It is even south of us here. It is one of the polar vortex things, which is a circular flow of frigid air that normally circles around the polar region. Well, now the jet stream is way south and the polar vortex has brought a whole lot of cold air our way. This is why it has gotten so cold. So now, what we are going to do is give you some new gear, and you are going to take it with you up to 13,000 feet and survive while the wind blows at 60 miles per hour. You may stay there for an undetermined period, probably a couple of days, simulating that you are on an op in the high mountains and get stuck in a snowstorm for a few days."

"You don't have to like it. In fact, you don't even have to do it. This is a volunteer operation, and nobody is going to get a bad mark in their record if they quit. In fact, this operation, including the training and whatever you do overseas, will not go into your service record. This one is off the books."

"You cannot talk about this operation with your buddies, your family, your spouse, or your favorite squeeze. This one is strictly classified. I imagine it is going to be important, or they would not have gone to all this trouble to bring you here."

"You are going to be issued a few layers of clothing. Some of it will include Lohtse Jackets, black color. Lohtse,

129

you know, is the fourth highest mountain in the world. Are you going there? I doubt it. Lohtse is connected to Mount Everest by the South Col. For you lowlanders who spent your whole life at the beach, the col is the pass that separates two peaks. Lohtse in Tibet means South Summit. In their language, Everest is called Chomo Lungma, meaning 'goddess mother.' That is a more fitting name for the highest peak in the world, because it shows proper reverence for the mountain."

"The particular magic of the Lohtse Jacket is that it is made of GORE-TEX, which is waterproof. You cannot predict what the weather will be like on this op, so it makes sense to make sure that you can stay dry. In the mountains, rain frequently comes at you horizontally, blown by high wind."

"A truly terrific insulator in the cold is down, goose down, from goose feathers. Goose down is wonderful in cold weather. Then you get it wet, and you freeze to death. Literally. Goose down loses all its insulating powers when you get it wet. So that's why we are going to give you a few layers of extra clothing for your survival training. We are also going to give you a lightweight pad that insulates you better when you sleep on the ground, so you don't freeze to death at night."

"To survive this next period of training you have to survive the nights. To survive the night, you have to get out of the wind. The wind is the killer. Get out of the wind and stay dry. Get some high calorie food in you. Stay hydrated.

That doesn't mean you drink a lot late in the day, because that would make you have to get up at night to pee."

"If your feet are cold, cover your head. Your head is the body's insulator. You lose 50% of the body's heat through your head. You have to cover your head and neck. Be careful with cold food. Cold food and drink will make your body temperature drop like a rock. Heat your food if you can. We gave you lightweight gas stoves. Use them. Be sure the gas stove has enough ventilation that you don't get a problem from carbon monoxide."

"If you are in a pine forest you can make good insulation from branches and pine needles, as long as they are dry. Up here there are no pine needles because there are no trees. There are also no bushes, as you have seen. So, you have to carry a lightweight insulating pad to put on the ground."

"We know your clothes sizes. So, go to the back of the trailer and the sergeant will issue you your new gear. Put it on. Make sure it is not too tight. Once you have your new gear, step outside, and get ready for a good climb."

BJ walked over to Stinko after they got all dressed up and stepped outside.

"Hey, Stinko, what are you going to do when this training stuff is over?"

"Me, I'm going to Taco Bell."

The instructor had to shout once they were outside because the wind was strong.

"You are going to sleep at the 13,000-foot level tonight. The wind up there is hellacious strong, so get out of the wind and try to stay dry. Try not to sweat while you are hiking. Take layers off. It is OK to be cold while you hike because it allows you to stay dry. You are not given a sleeping bag for this exercise. You get parachute material. You make a sleeping bag out of the parachute silk, and you make a makeshift tent out of the same material. You can cut it with your knives."

"There is just one rule that you have to follow. You cannot go any lower than the campsite we show you. That will be at 13,000 feet. You can go up; you cannot go down. You go lower, you flunk this op, and you are disqualified. DQ! That's DQ, Jack, you got that? If you DQ you are outa here. If you are outa here you do not talk about what you were doing. You get a court-martial for talking about this op. If you aren't military, you won't get a court-martial, but you get a trial and you could go to prison. Got that?"

Within the first minute of the climb Stinko and Abdul were taking off layers of clothing. BJ followed their example. Not everyone did.

The instructor drove an all-terrain vehicle up a cinder path road to the 13,000-foot level. The cold was terrible. Most of the people were picking a place to spend the night. BJ looked around and saw Stinko and Abdul walking slowly up hill, away from the campsite. BJ watched them go and just stayed where he was. He and his partner were exhausted from climbing. They could not be talked into more climbing for any reason.

Stinko and Abdul hiked slowly for about a quarter mile

and walked over a ridge. Beyond the ridge was a gentle downslope. They got to the bottom of the downslope and dug a depression into the ground, which was still dry. They built up a wall of sorts from the rocks and cinders in the area. The wall was to be their windbreak during the night. The windspeed here was half what it was at the campsite that everyone was using. Stinko and Abdul made sure their bodies were dry before they put on their cold weather gear. Then they covered their heads.

They fired up their gas stove and ate dinner slowly. They sliced up the parachute that they were given and tied a knot in the bottom to make a sleeping bag. There was enough silk left to use as a loose wrapper around themselves. They put their ground pads in the low spot, put their makeshift sleeping bags inside the big wrapper, and put that on top of the pads, and climbed into the sleeping bags.

"Hey Abdul?"

"Yeah."

"This is cold."

"Yeah."

"Let's put one sleeping bag inside the other to make two layers. It will be warmer. Then let's climb into the sleeping bag back-to-back," Stinko suggested.

"OK. It may be warmer than this. This is bad," Abdul replied.

"Hey Abdul?"

"Yeah."

"Don't fart."

"Hey Stinko?"

"Yeah."

"Go screw yourself."

After a while they slept. Most of the people couldn't sleep. Too cold and too weird because of the howling wind.

At seven o'clock the next morning the big ATV with the instructors and a doctor drove up the mountain to the campsite. The doctor diagnosed six cases of serious frostbite. Their training was over. The people with frostbite were disqualified. Several of the others had minor cases of frostnip. After warm food their fingers and toes tingled like crazy from edema, but they were OK. The frostbite cases had severe edema once the circulation returned to their appendages. If they had stayed in the severe cold any longer, they could have lost fingers or toes or both. They were driven down to the 10,000-foot level and medevacked out by helicopter.

For training the next day they hiked down to the 10,000-foot level and hiked back up to the 13,000-foot level. The wind was still howling. After the second night six people dropped out. Twenty-four people started. Now there were twelve.

Bern was still there.

The next day they did some training on shooting at various distances, downhill with a steep slope. They all left their packs in a circle about a quarter mile away from the makeshift rifle range. When they got back to their packs, Bern was already there, going through Stinko's bag.

"What are you doing?" Stinko asked. "What the hell?"

"Get out of my way, dick wad!" Bern shouted.

Stinko pulled Bern toward him roughly, then slammed a leg behind Bern and shoved him to the ground.

"What the hell is going on over there?" an instructor shouted.

"This jerk took the food out of my pack. Look for yourself."

They did. In his pack Bern had his own food plus Stinko's food and Abdul's food. Stinko's pack and Abdul's pack had no food at all.

"You are out of here, soldier!" they shouted at Bern. "You just disqualified yourself from this mission."

"Yeah, well, who gives a rat's ass about this mission anyway?" Bern mumbled.

Bern shouted at the instructor, "Why do you let this raghead compete anyway? He isn't even an American."

"Pack your gear soldier. Your teammate goes too. As for you, you are lucky you don't get a court-martial."

"That's the benefit of this super-secret hush hush mission," Bern whispered to his teammate. It's so secret they won't report me."

There were five teams left.

"Eat lunch and we are going back to the rifle range this afternoon," the instructor directed the group.

When they finished at the rifle range, they got an ominous warning from the instructor:

"Tomorrow is exam day, ladies. Get some rest tonight. You are going to need it."

They were still at 13,000 feet, but the wind was mercifully light.

The next morning, after some chow, the instructor said, "Get your packs, rifles, and helmets. Make sure your socks are dry. Fall in here in ten minutes."

There were four teams consisting of two men and one team consisting of two women.

"OK, ladies. You will hike down to the 10,000-foot level. You will draw your ammunition there. Two rounds per person. You will then hike up here to the rifle range that is here at the 13,000-foot level. You will be timed. You will shoot two rounds per person. The first shot will be a body shot at the center mass of the body on the target. The second shot will be a head shot at the same target. As you know, there are circles on the targets, ten points for the center, nine points for the next ring, and so on down to one point. You will be scored by an instructor. There are ten targets, one for each person. The first team up here gets to pick what two shooting positions they want to use. The second team gets to pick the next two shooting positions. We put down mats for you to shoot from. We will pull the mats from your shooting position when you are done, so the shooting positions don't get reused. The last team to get here gets what is left."

"After you are done shooting you high tail it over to the campsite that is here at the 13,000-foot level. You are still on the clock, so move it. Sergeant Kominski is at the campsite and will give you a pie plate that has your name on it. You hike over there to get the plate because that gets you safely clear of the rifle range and shows the instructors that you are not cutting corners. You will take your plate down to the 10,000-foot level and trade it in for two rounds of ammunition per person. You will hike back up here and shoot two rounds again. One round goes to the center mass of the body, one round goes to the head. You are required to have a helmet, a pack, and a rifle for the entire evolution. When you finish your last shot, run over to Sergeant Kominski at the campsite to record your time."

"What you are shooting today is match grade ammo. There is no difference between these rounds."

"There is water, sports drinks, and granola up here at the camp. There's food down there at the bottom where you draw your ammo. Eat. Don't get out of energy. Drink. You will need it. You can carry as much water or sports drink as you like. Remember you are going down and up two times. You are obviously going down 3000 feet and up 3000 feet twice, and you shoot for record twice. Pace yourselves because this is likely to take ten hours. Good luck."

"We will start this exercise when everyone has their gear on and has filled their canteen with as much liquid as they think they will need."

Stinko and Abdul knew they could outclimb the others. They didn't know if they could descend faster. They were about to find out.

The GG Team with Gomez and Gujar descended faster

than anybody. They drew their ammo, got some food, water, and had a good head start on the ascent. Stinko and Abdul had a five-minute deficit to make up, which they did by the time they were halfway up the climb. They got to the rifle range with a good lead.

"Wait," Abdul said. "If we shoot now, we shake too much."

"OK. We can shoot whenever you are ready," Stinko replied.

They waited several minutes. The GG Team was just getting to the rifle range when Abdul took his first shot. Abdul finished his second shot, then Stinko did his shooting. He waited for Abdul to finish before he started shooting, to avoid distractions from the noise. They hustled over to the campsite to pick up their plates.

The two men on the GG Team were really pleased that they had caught up to their rivals. Gomez got on the mat, took a few breaths, and realized that he was still heaving from heavy breathing. He waited one minute, then another.

"What are you waiting for? Come on!" his partner Gujar shouted.

Gomez took a few more breaths to calm himself. It wasn't enough. His first shot hit the target in the center mass, but in an outer ring for a low score. His second shot was a miss.

His partner Gujar fared no better.

None of the teams that followed gave themselves enough time to settle down for the shot.

The instructor thought about telling the teams to slow down for the final round of shooting. He decided against it. It was an exam, and there wouldn't be any coaches when they got where they were going.

The GG Team was a minute ahead of Stinko and Abdul when they drew their ammo at the bottom. It didn't matter. The team of Stinko and Abdul had a fifteen-minute lead when they finished the climb and arrived at the rifle range. They spent ten minutes of that time calming down. They put their bullets in the target. Nobody matched their shooting. Nobody matched their time.

"OK, people, get your gear and get into the big truck. We'll give you a ride down to the 10,000-foot level. You can see your scores and times when you get to the bottom. You can sleep on a cot tonight."

The shooting scores for Stinko and Abdul were super. The KK ladies team took second place. The GG Team was third. The scores for the other two teams weren't so good. Since they finished this phase of training, their dinner was catered from a restaurant way down at sea level. It was fantastic, compared to what they had been getting.

The Sergeant Major addressed the group:

"You have one more week of training, then we will announce which teams are the 'Go Teams' and which are the backups. After we announce the teams, you will be told what your assignments will be after this op completes. You will not be returning to the same command that you came from before."

"When you leave this place, you will not and I repeat

NOT talk about the training you have been doing, and you will not talk about the operation that some of you will participate in. If you talk, you will be in violation of the criminal code of the United States by providing material support to terrorism. The reason you are not returning to your old commands is that fewer people will ask you what you were doing. If people ask, you will tell them nothing. If your new boss asks, you will tell him or her that you were supposed to test fire a new weapon, but in fact all you did was shoot some of the old stuff like the M14, M16, AK47 and AK74. You will in fact be shooting those weapons during the next week and given classes on their capabilities. These classes will have written exams, which you will pass, or you will never leave here. The AK74 uses the 5.45x39mm cartridge instead of the 7.62x39mm cartridge in the AK47. You will be expected to know that. The AK74 is more accurate, lighter in weight, and cheaper to manufacture. The barrel is different. There was some redesign of the gas block."

"The M14 replaced the M1 Garand that was used by the U.S. military in WWII and Korea. If you compared the M14 to the AK47, the M14 was more powerful, more accurate, and could shoot farther."

"The M16 replaced the M14 as the primary weapon for the U.S. military in Vietnam. Although the M14 shoots the 7.62mm cartridge farther and more accurately than the M16, the M16 spreads automatic fire over a larger area, and more rapidly, and the M16 uses the 5.56mm cartridge, which is lighter and allows the soldier to carry more ammunition."

During the last week of training, they did a lot of hiking and shooting. They spent enough time in class to learn about military weapons and pass the exams. The snipers were given their weapon of choice this week and were able to practice daily for hours. The U.S. Army people chose the Army M24 Sniper Weapon, the standard sniper rifle since 1988. It uses the Remington 700 rifle, weighs 16 pounds fully loaded with scope and sling. Its cartridge is the 7.62x51mm NATO round.

Although the U.S. Marine snipers prefer the M40, nobody selected it. Abdul chose his old favorite, the Dragunov Sniper Rifle, Russian manufacture, made by Kalashnikov. It uses the 7.62x54mm cartridge. It is not the same cartridge that the Army rifle uses, but it was thought that snipers would not need to share ammunition. If necessary, ammo could be shared between everyone carrying the M4, with the 5.56x45mm rounds.

At the end of the week, they learned their fate. There had been a decision at high levels to take three teams to Afghanistan, and to keep the remaining teams in reserve. The three "Go Teams" consisted of four men and two women. The finalists were Stinko, Abdul, Kristen, Kaamisha, Gomez, and Gujar.

There was a possibility that one more team of women would be brought to Afghanistan, to gather intelligence. That decision had not yet been finalized.

An instructor told them that they would go by bus to Kona, on the west coast of the big island of Hawaii, then catch flights to Honolulu, and proceed to destinations stateside. They were authorized a 36-hour layover in the States before departing for Bagram Air Base, Afghanistan.

"We will provide flights for you. Give us your stateside address and phone number. We will have your schedule in a couple of hours. After you have your schedule, you can call whoever you want using the telephones over there. After your layover wherever you wish to be in the States, you need to get to JFK airport. I am handing out a sheet of paper to each of you that says be at the USO Center, JFK Airport, Terminal 5, at 4:00 PM Eastern Daylight Time, on March 26. We will pick you up there, at the USO, at JFK Airport, and take you to McGuire Air Force Base in New Jersey. From there we will get you on a military flight to Bagram Air Base, Afghanistan. Your weapons will be on the military flight with you when you leave McGuire."

"If you are going to be late arriving at JFK because of a problem with your flight, call me at the phone number you see on that sheet of paper. Call anytime. There is also a phone number for an office at the Pentagon that you can call anytime, day or night. They can get in touch with me."

"The USO stands for United Service Organizations. They have a lounge there and food. To use the USO Center you must have a military ID or a DoD, Department of Defense, ID. I am passing out DoD IDs to the Dari language speakers. Have it with you when you show up at the USO Center at JFK airport. I will be there to meet you."

"Put your cold weather gear and equipment in these

duffel bags we are giving you. They will be on your flight with you when you leave McGuire. I will meet you at the USO and go with you to McGuire Air Force Base. Make sure your duffel bag has everything you need and check it again when we get to McGuire."

"We don't want people asking questions when you travel. We have civilian clothes for you in the back of the trailer. If someone asks you what you do, say you work in supply. If they ask again, tell them it is boring and don't say anymore."

Kaamisha was pleased. JFK Airport was near her home in New York.

Ronnie knew that he would stop over in Chicago to see Jennifer. He immediately thought of Abdul's fiancée, Meena.

"Abdul, can you get Meena to fly to Chicago so you can see her? You can stay in Jennifer' apartment, or we will get a room for you at a hotel."

Abdul agreed. Once they had their flight schedules, they all needed to use the telephones at the same time. Somehow, they managed.

Kona, Hawaii

In the morning the trainees got a bus ride down to Kona. They had a few hours to kill before the flight from Kona to Honolulu. Stinko and Abdul went down the coast to see the place where they start and finish the Ironman Triathlon World Championship races. As they walked up from the beach, they saw someone staggering out of one of the local bars. It was none other than the redneck Bern.

"Hey! Hey raghead! I got something for you!" Bern shouted.

Abdul and Stinko kept walking.

"Hey raghead! Bern grabbed Abdul's collar. Stinko struck Bern's wrist hard with an upward stroke that freed Abdul. They kept walking.

Stinko was pretty sure that this evolution would not turn out well for Bern, since there was a cop in uniform watching them.

"Hey raghead, I'm talking to you! Don't you walk away from me!"

They kept walking away.

Bern ran up to them, reached into his jacket, and pulled out a pistol.

Abdul glanced up and to the right, and Bern followed his glance. Abdul struck a hard blow to Bern's wrist, causing the gun to fly skyward. Nobody was injured. Abdul drove the base of his palm into Bern's nose, which knocked him out.

The policeman approached them and asked them to stay. The cop kicked the gun clear of Bern, picked up the gun, and put it in an evidence bag. He made sure that Bern was breathing and called for backup. The cop took their names and addresses. The policeman asked if they knew the man with the gun.

Stinko explained, "We were here for some survival training with the military, and this guy stole our food. He got caught and was expelled from the training. We had nothing against him at the time. Just now we were trying to walk away from him, and he kept following us. Three times we tried to walk away from him."

"Yeah, I saw that. Are these phone numbers good for you?"

"Yes, sir."

The cop gave each of them a pad of paper and a pen. "Write down a statement of what happened. Print your name and sign the statement. Include your phone number where you can be reached."

They complied.

"I'm going to let you go. I saw what happened. We will take this guy in and see if he has a permit for the weapon, where he got it, and so on. You can go now."

Chapter 9

The Pentagon

When the Pentagon received the go-ahead from the White House to run the op, the team members were still on the mountain in Hawaii, training at high elevation. They did not want the operators to lose their acclimation to the high altitude. The team members started to work with sniper rifles and the M4 carbines. They started hiking wearing helmets and flak jackets. They worked on battlefield medicine. The Sergeant Major flew back to Virginia to be available for planning sessions in the Pentagon.

The Pentagon people did not have good intel on the target, so they did what they always do in these situations: they held a meeting. The three-star, Lieutenant General Tuttle, kicked it off.

"We have a green light to run this op. What we have always done at this stage is move our team to Bagram Air Base in Afghanistan and wait for good intel. Is that what we want to do now?"

After a moment when nobody replied, Sergeant Major Johnson spoke up. "General, we have normally waited for some intel, then moved a team out from Bagram, usually by helo. It is usually a couple of hours later the team gets into position, announcing its arrival to the bad guys by a noisy helo flight. Why don't we have our teams in staging places, with their own vehicles, so they can be activated without a noisy helo flight?"

"Another thing, general. We will need the helos for the exfil. Our guys get on site, make their shot, make their escape, and need a pickup. We are going to need those Air Force helo drivers to be selected early enough so they can work with our guys when they get to Bagram. I want them to practice together and get used to each other's voices. We need to make sure their radios are compatible, and make sure they use the same terminology. They need to be able to describe pickup points that the helo drivers can find. They have to know how to get into and out of the helo. I'll bet that some of the native speakers have never been in a helo. Let's correct that with some training at Bagram Air Base. Also, all our operators need to learn the altitude limits on the helos. There is no sense in calling up a rescue from some altitude the helo can't handle. We also better do a little practice with our teams to help them judge elevation."

"You got it, Sergeant Major. I'll get the names of the pilots to you ASAP and we will arrange a date for a rendezvous with our teams when they finish training."

"General, I want to talk to your aviation specialist for a minute."

"The major is right here. Fire away."

The Sergeant Major addressed the major. "Which helicopter are we going to use?"

"We considered the UH-1 Huey and the UH-60 Black

Hawk. The Huey has a service ceiling of 12,600 feet. The Blackhawk has a service ceiling of 19,000 feet."

"So, it will be the Black Hawk. How many does the Air Force have?"

"Very few. Used for medevac."

"How about the U.S. Army?"

"Like 2000."

"Well, the Army guys on this op on the ground will likely feel more comfortable with Army pilots to pick them up."

"What about the gunships?"

"They have the Pave Hawk helicopters. They are Air Force. They have been used for medevac too."

"What's the service ceiling?"

"Like 14,000 feet."

"Why is it 14,000 feet when the Black Hawk is 19,000 feet?"

"The Pave Hawk has an auxiliary fuel tank, plus guns, plus chaff, plus flares. More weight."

"Well, the UH-60 Black Hawk with its 19,000-foot service ceiling is a safer bet for this op for the exfil. But as a gunship the Pave Hawk is a possibility. What about the C-130 gunship?"

"That's Air Force and so is the Pave Hawk. Their AC-130 is the gunship that is well-liked by the Air Force Special Operations Command. It's armed to the teeth, can transit to the op area at 300 knots (about 345 mph), has a service ceiling of 25,000 feet (7620m), and can stay up there forever."

The major said, "I wouldn't rule out the Pave Hawk helicopter for the exfil. The Pave Hawk is a special version of the Black Hawk that has auxiliary fuel tanks, so it has longer range. It has chaff, flares, missile detectors, radar detectors, and guns on each side that shoot 4000 rounds per minute. Those are Air Force birds."

"Can we get both? Pave Hawks, and the AC-130?"

The General answered that one.

"Sergeant Major, you can get anything you need. I can just about guarantee it. Let's get crews and aircraft lined up for this. And maintenance crews, and billeting, and transportation, and spare parts, and extra chow at the dining facilities, and whatever else these crews will need."

The General pointed to his aid, who said, "I'm on it General. We will stage them out of Bagram."

"If we let the operators move into country with cars instead of having them stage out of Bagram, they will need reliable radios or cell phone coverage, or both, so we can activate them. They also would need vehicles that don't draw attention to them, right? They could probably live in the town. It is not like these towns have never seen Americans before."

"Major, remind me how the chaff and flares work on the Pave Hawk."

"That's totally cool. The flares are in pods on the side of the aircraft, pointed down. The flares are fired to confuse heat seeker missiles. The chaff is fired from pods that point up, also mounted on the side of the helo. The chaff is strips of metal like aluminum foil and gets shot through the tail rotor. That disperses it into a cloud, making a target for missile radar."

The Sergeant Major called Sergeant Rogers and had him meet him in his office in the Pentagon.

"Sergeant Rogers, I'm going to need you for an op. We are going to Kandahar."

"Kandahar? Me and who else?"

"Kristen Kraska and Kaamisha."

"Kristen and Kaamisha? The KK Team in Kandahar? OK KKKK!"

"Rogers, you are weird."

"What's our job?"

"The women get the intel, just as you suggested. They provide it to us, and we move the shooters."

Chapter 10

Chicago

Ronnie and Abdul got a direct flight from Honolulu to Chicago O'Hare. Jennifer, the love of Ronnie's life, picked them up at the airport. Jennifer got a crushing hug.

After a great hug and a big kiss, Ronnie realized that standing a few feet back from them was his best friend, Jack Russell.

"Jack!"

"Stinko! You really are alive!"

"Jack, this is a surprise! I never thought I'd see you here!"

"I never thought I'd see you alive!"

Stinko got a big hug.

"Holy smokes! Jack, great to see you! This is my partner, Abdul. Abdul, this is Jack Russell, the guy I was telling you about."

Jack observed a Middle Eastern man, bearded, olive skin, with alert, dark eyes. Abdul extended his hand. "Jack," he said.

"Abdul. Pleased to meet you! You actually have to work with this nutcase?"

"Yes, when I can keep up with him. Sometimes it is not easy."

"Yeah, I can believe that!"

"Abdul, what Airline is Meena on?" Jennifer asked.

"She is on American flight. Due to arrive 30 minutes ago."

"That's terminal 3. You guys came in on United, terminal 1. Jump in the car, we can go get her," Jennifer said.

Meena carried a small carry-on bag, had a scarf on her head, and looked great. Abdul jumped out of the car when he saw her and gave her the best hug of his life. They climbed into the car.

"Where are we going?" Abdul asked.

"My place, for dinner," Jennifer replied. "I realize you just crossed five time zones, but you gotta eat."

"Abdul, do you like pizza?" Jennifer asked.

"Sure," he replied. "No pork."

"We can do a cheese pizza, or beef. Meena, we have lots to eat. You OK with pizza, salad, and lots of fruit?"

"Yes. Fine." Meena obviously had learned some English.

"We are going to want a lot of protein and vegetables while we are here," Stinko said. He could be counted on to think of food all the time.

"And you will be here for how long?" Jen asked.

"Thirty-six hours."

"Wham, bam, thank you, mam," was Jennifer's reply.

"Well, I didn't write the schedule," Stinko answered.

"It's OK. I'm not complaining."

Jennifer had inherited a house but sold it and put the proceeds from the sale into mutual funds. She lived in an apartment.

"My neighbor gave me her apartment to use while you guys are in town. Abdul can stay there while you are in town. We all are getting together for dinner, though. Jack's girlfriend Sue will come too, OK?"

Ronnie had known Sue pretty much for his whole life. They had grown up together. Sue and Jack had been a couple for as long as he could remember.

"That's great."

The traffic was the usual heavy stuff all the way home. Jack called Sue on his cell phone as they drove. Sue pulled up at Jennifer's place as they arrived.

Abdul noticed that the women here were casually dressed, wearing no head scarves. The women seemed to do everything, including driving cars. He had seen some women pilots in the airport. He thought, "I would like Meena to be able to have that kind of freedom. If I had a daughter, I would like that for her, too." He thought of the men he had worked with over the years. Most of them preferred their women to be in the home, doing what they considered to be proper for a female. He had seen that for his own mother.

When Sue got to the parking lot at Jennifer's apartment complex, she parked the car and climbed out. When she saw Ronnie, she ran over to him and gave him a big hug.

"Oh man, Ronnie, we thought we lost you!" Tears streamed down her face. "Jen said so much nice stuff about you at your funeral! You are going to have to walk on water for a while to get caught up to your image!" Sue said.

"Well, I did come back from the dead. That must count for something!" Stinko replied.

"How did you do that, by the way? I have got to hear all about this," Sue said.

"Well, it is a long story."

"Well, it's a long night."

Jen started the oven the moment they got into her apartment. She gave a key to Abdul and walked with him and Meena to the apartment they would stay in that night. This apartment was a couple of doors down the hall from hers.

When they walked into the apartment together, Meena looked at Abdul. Her eyes were big as saucers.

"Abdul, we are going to stay in this apartment alone together," she whispered.

"Yes. Is it OK?" Abdul asked, hoping she was comfortable with the idea.

"I'll do it with you. You know I want to marry you. I wanted it before you asked me. Can we get married here?" Meena asked.

"Maybe not in the one day we have. Will you marry me when we get back?" he asked.

"Yes."

They all got together in the kitchen. Jennifer had pizza, plus two cooked chickens, bananas, apples, carrots, broccoli, tossed salad with onions, tomatoes, croutons, fruit salad, watermelon, cantaloupe, nuts, avocados, and orange slices. This was Ronnie's standard fare since he became a high-altitude endurance nut. She provided beer and wine, along with sweet tea, lemonade, water, coke, Pepsi, 7Up, and some root beer. Abdul and Meena liked the sweet tea.

They had a great dinner. Abdul made an announcement.

"Ronnie, I have something to say. Meena and I will get married when we get back from this job."

"Congratulations! Congratulations!" Everyone offered their congratulations.

Jennifer looked at Ronnie. He said, "Jennifer?"

They didn't say a word. They just got up and kissed.

Sue looked at Jack. "What are you waiting for Jack Russell?"

Jack grabbed her hand and said, "Sue. You know I would do anything for you."

"That isn't a proposal, but I'll take it," Sue said.

Sue and Jack excused themselves and left early. Abdul tried to excuse himself as well, but Jennifer said, "Just a minute, Abdul. I need to talk to you, both of you."

Ronnie, Abdul, Meena, and Jen sat around the kitchen table.

Jennifer was concerned about this whole operation. "I'm afraid you won't come back. I buried what I thought was you once. I just want to know that they aren't sending you out there without all the help you can get. The best equipment. He best training. You need to use technology of this century to keep you alive."

"Well, Ronnie started out. We use satellite imagery, sure. We have the best aircraft and helicopters. I'm not getting into our entry and exfil methods. The equipment is ultra-light. The helmets are Kevlar, the boots are super. We have flak jackets. Our cold weather gear is super."

"Abdul?"

"The navigation is good, really good. GPS. The cameras are good. The communication radios are unbelievable. I never see radios like these. We have every weapon we want. I can choose what I want, and they give it to me."

"What about the new stuff? She asked."

They looked at her.

"That's what I was afraid of. On TV I saw little birds, manmade, that can fly around and bug a house. You got them? These birds are robots. Miniature robots. They look and fly like birds. They also have some that look like insects. You could bug a house with them. You could find out who is in the house and what they say. You could have machines that program the density altitude, so your shot is not screwed up by thin air."

"Density altitude?" Stinko asked.

"Jack is a pilot, dummy. We talk. You know he calculates the length of his takeoff roll based on field elevation, temperature, and humidity. If any of the three of them increases, the density altitude increases, and the takeoff roll length increases. You guys don't factor that in?"

She was getting blank stares.

"Well? Do you have rangefinders?"

"Sure, but sometimes just a good scope is enough."

"You got night vision goggles?"

"Yeah."

Comm gear? Do you have to shout at each other?

"No. We have radios, like Abdul said."

"Are they encrypted?"

"I'm not going to talk about our comm gear with you."

"OK. I just want to know that you have the best gear you can get so there is the best chance you will come back."

"I'll come back. We will come back. Count on it."

Abdul and Meena left the apartment. Jen and Ronnie cleaned up the kitchen, turned out the lights, and walked into the bedroom. Ronnie shut the door behind him.

"Ronnie, do you think you are doing the right thing?"

"You mean by going to Afghanistan?"

She nodded.

"If not me, then who?" Ronnie said. "The Taliban are in Afghanistan. They enforce sharia law. Some of them rape and kill women. Sometimes they behead women who walk in town alone or won't cover their heads."

"You aren't going to change them," Jennifer said.

"I know. They aren't the problem. The problem is Al Qaeda, and the Taliban give them a safe place to train and recruit."

She looked at him.

"There have been several Islamic caliphates since the end of the seventh century. Under a caliphate there is one Islamic ruler, the caliph. After Muhammad died, they spread their dominion from across all northern Africa, into southern Spain, across the Middle East, through Turkey and Greece, across Asia and out into Indonesia. The Al

Qaeda want to re-establish the caliphate in all those places and spread it worldwide. They kill any infidel. They even kill Muslims who will not use violence to further their goals. It's not right."

"Why is that your concern?"

"It's not right to foist your idea of religion on someone else."

"You have been reading. I am beginning to think that you really could be a teacher when this is all over."

"Jen. Come to me."

Jen and Ronnie melted into each other. He could feel her warm body pressed against his. He stroked her face, her hair. He wrapped his arms around her and felt her cheek against his. He smelled her fragrant hair.

"Jen?"

"Hmm?"

"The time I am with you is the best time in my life. I would walk across a fire for you."

"I know you would Ronnie. I don't want that."

He looked at her.

"Just come back Ronnie."

Chapter 11

Bagram Air Base, Afghanistan

Lieutenant General Tuttle, US Army, called the meeting to order. It was the same three-star general who had been with the mission since day one.

"I am Lieutenant General Tuttle. I thank you for volunteering for the mission. This is Sergeant Major Johnson. The Sergeant Major completed a tour in Afghanistan recently and speaks Dari. The Sergeant Major has been with this program from its inception. He and a few other people hand-picked the operators for the mission. He has the best perspective on how to run this operation. The Sergeant Major has the complete support of both me and everyone above me all the way up to and including the White House. If you cannot follow the lead of the Sergeant Major, see me at the end of this brief and we will see that you are excused. Sergeant Major, it's your group."

They were in a trailer at Bagram Air Base, Afghanistan. The air base is in northeast Afghanistan at an elevation of 4895 feet (1492 meters), with two runways. One of the runways is 11,819 feet long (3602m), long enough to handle large aircraft.

The group was impressed that a three-star general had kicked off the meeting. In attendance were Stinko, Abdul, Kristen, Kaamisha, Gomez, Gujar, the pilots and crew of two Black Hawk helicopters, the pilots and crew of two

Pave Hawk attack helicopters, and the pilots and crew of one AC-130 gunship. Also in attendance were two backup teams that had completed all the training at both the Army Mountain Warfare School in Vermont and the training in Hawaii. The backup teams were comprised of one team of men and one team of women. The operators were surprised to see the second team of women, who had experienced problems with the cold during the survival drill, yet here they were.

The Sergeant Major spoke clearly, "OK people. We were ordered to come to this place to get ready to go after a Taliban leader who has given us a lot of trouble. Everything that we discuss from this point forward will be Top Secret. The reason for the high classification is that the target is designated as a high value target (HVT). We have gone after this guy at least three times before, with Army, Marines, and SEALs. None of those ops worked. The operation you are on now has been given the highest classification by the Defense Priorities Allocations System (DPAS). That means if you need something in the way of equipment or supplies, you should have it. If you don't have it, let me know, and I'll get it for you."

"I'm Sergeant Major Johnson," he said for the benefit of the aircrews who were meeting him. "I've been with this program from its inception. I will be your point of contact for supplies, gear, billeting, food, schedules, and whatever you need. You need something, let me know. You think we are missing the ball on something, let me know. Army

Master Sergeant Josephine Storm is my assistant. Raise your hand, Josie. If you need something or have some concern, talk to me, or talk to Josie, OK?"

"I'm going to let Sergeant Rogers here show you short film clips to explain the capabilities of the three different aircraft that we are using. That's primarily for the benefit of you operators. After the aircraft movies, we are going to brief you on the training that these operators have been getting. When we are done with the brief, we'll ask you to introduce yourselves."

They finished the film clips and the brief. The Sergeant Major walked to the front of the room again. "Let's go around the room now and introduce ourselves. Tell us the nickname you want to go by while you work with us, and what outfit you are working with. I want you on first name basis while you work this op."

After the introductions, the Sergeant Major resumed speaking.

"Our target is named Borst. Sergeant Rogers projected a few photos of Borst on the screen. Borst operates with a band of from 20 to 75 men. He was last seen several weeks ago in the vicinity of Kandahar. If we get good intel on his position, we will react accordingly. His people have used US-manufactured M4 and M16 rifles, well-maintained Soviet-era weapons such as the AK47, the AK74, RPGs, IEDs, and surface to air missiles like our stinger missiles."

"We are going to use every asset at our disposal to find Borst or his men. Every asset. We are also going to use our operators. It is planned to use the women as intel collectors in Kandahar. We are going to ask the local speakers on our women teams, and that means all the women teams, to buy fruits and local foods from the local markets. Become a familiar customer in the markets. Shop daily. Keep your ears open. We will give you a few questions that we want you to ask. After you become familiar with the local sellers, you can ask the questions. You can ask other questions that you think will help us. The objective is to find Borst or his soldiers."

"Sergeant Major? Gomez asked. If our target is down around Kandahar, which is like a 5000-foot elevation, why did we train all the time from 10,000 feet to 13,000 feet (3962m)?"

"Good question. No question is a bad one, by the way. We trained at high elevation because Borst has been known to move to northeast Afghanistan when he gets spooked. Meaning, if he thinks he's being hunted and they are getting close, he heads for the hills. Unfortunately, this country has the mountain range called the Hindu Kush, which goes up to 25,000 feet. There are lots of mountains higher than 20,000 feet (6096m). Even the lower slopes on mountains like that are at very, very high elevations. Hence you had training at the high elevations. Does that answer your question?"

"Yes. Thank you."

"I understand that the service ceiling of the Pave Hawk is around 14,000 feet, the service ceiling of the Black Hawk is around 19,000 feet, and the service ceiling of the AC-130 is around 25,000 feet. I will not ask you to operate at or near your service ceiling if I can help it."

"A service ceiling means the aircraft can still climb at a rate of 50 feet per minute with one engine out. The helicopters have two engines. The AC-130 has four. The term 'service ceiling' applies to all our aircraft. Nevertheless, the point is that we will not ask you to go to your service ceiling if we can help it."

"Pilots from the Black Hawk helos, raise your hand please. You were asked to bring some cheat sheets with your standard terminology, right? Do you have them? Good. Please provide that to Sergeant Rogers here. He is going to make copies for everyone. We are going to start training by talking in small groups between the air crews and the operators. You will see on the screen five scenarios, where the crew on the ground requests a pickup based on GPS positions. We have grid maps to use to identify the positions you will be picked up at. We are going to do an exercise after you get familiar with the terminology. We are going to see if the aircrew writes down the correct position based on what the operators tell them.

"Operators will eat meals with the helicopter aircrews that can do pickups. That is not voluntary. That is part of the op. Get to know each other. Get to know the voice. Get to know how they talk."

"Before we start this phase of training, we will take a ten-minute break. There are bagels, coffee, tea, and water in the back of the room. Don't expect to get doughnuts, because the sugary foods cause a sugar rush for an hour which is followed by an insulin rush and a blood sugar crash which lasts for hours. That has been reported again and again in aviation accident reports. Low blood sugar has been a factor in the aircraft accidents over and over again. We are going to talk about nutrition while you are here. Your body is an engine, and your food is your fuel. Put in the good stuff and you can thrive."

"OK, let's take the break. Ten minutes."

Before starting the break Kristen and Kaamisha approached Sergeant Major Johnson.

"Sergeant Major, if we are going to do our work in the city, why did you have us train at 13,000 feet and compete with rifles?"

"Good question, Kristen. You know, it has been famously said that no plan survives initial contact with the enemy. We are only going to use two teams as shooters. That's four men. If anything happens to any one of the men on either team, that team is out of action as far as we are concerned. Then, your team is their replacement. The other team you see in the room isn't the first replacement. Your team is the first replacement. You two won the competition. You become the shooters. We are using women in the cities because we think they will be less threatening and less likely to cause suspicion. Does that answer your question?"

After the break they practiced using standard terminology and speaking to each other. Each team member of the operators got a turn speaking. After that session they got coffee again, and the flight crews were asked to report to their aircraft and be ready to show their aircraft to the operators.

While the flyers were headed down to the flight line, the operators got to watch a ten-minute movie that explains how a helicopter flies. It explained basics, like the collective is at the left hand of the pilot. If you want to go up, you pull the collective up. If you want to go down, you push the collective down. The cyclic is between the pilot's knees. If you want to go forward, you push the cyclic forward. To go back, pull the cyclic back. To go left, push left. To go right, push right. The rudders make the nose of the helo go left or right, rotating about a vertical axis. The movie explained that the tail rotor is there to overcome the torque generated by the rotors.

After the brief, the operators were ready to look for the flight controls when they followed the flyers down to the flight line. They all went down to the flight line. All of them. Men, women, everybody.

After the operators got their initial familiarization briefing from the aircrews, they strapped into the seats in back of the Black Hawk helicopter and tightened the harness. Then they released the harness and got out. Then they did it again, five times. Then they were asked to walk 100 meters away from the Black Hawk, run to the aircraft, climb into the helo, sit down, and strap in. They were timed from the moment the first operator touched the helo. Then they repeated the process in the Pave Hawk helicopter.

"Why are we doing this in the Pave Hawk?"

"Because we don't know which helo will get to you first."

"But we are supposed to use the Black Hawk."

"What if the Black Hawk has an engine failure and has to RTB (Return to Base)? What if a bird like a hawk flies into the engine, the engine fails, and the aircraft can't make it to your elevation? What if the Pave Hawk just happens to be in position to get you?"

"What's the difference? Why practice this drill in both airplanes?"

"The Pave Hawk has an extra fuel tank. Its compartment is different."

They practiced this basic maneuver day and night until they could do it with their eyes closed. Any fear they had of the aircraft was dispelled by then.

They practiced using the basic terminology that the aircrews provided. They started when they were seated together in the trailer. Later they practiced communicating using radios when they were out of sight of each other. They practiced when there was background noise. They practiced when the teammate who spoke Dari was the one doing the talking.

When the Sergeant Major was satisfied that they had mastered the basics, the teams started flying. They recovered the operators from positions using a GPS position on a map. They practiced on flat terrain. They practiced on sloped terrain. They went to the mountains north of the air base and practiced there, at high elevations.

They got a device that encoded their GPS position and used that to relay their position to the aircrew. They couldn't make it work beyond a few miles. They decided to use the maps and radios instead.

They considered using multiple maps, so that the enemy couldn't figure out where they were if they had heard their transmissions. They considered having five maps, labeled Alfa, Bravo, Charley, Delta, and Echo. Using the five maps they could broadcast their position saying something like "Alfa 37," meaning use map Alfa and we are in box 37. They considered it. They considered that the operators could be exhausted, scared, shot at, wounded, at night, needing a rescue, and having to get the right map out of their pack, hold it in the wind, not allow the other four maps to blow away or get ripped in a strong mountain wind. They decided to limit it to just one map with a clear plastic wrapper to keep it dry. KISS – Keep It Simple, Stupid.

"OK people. You noticed that these helicopters have a FRIES bar, a Fast Rope Insertion Extraction System, which the para rescuers, called PJs, use. You won't use the FRIES bar because it is for the soldiers to go from the helo to the ground. However, you may use the hoist that the Pave Hawk and the Black Hawk have. They can hoist you up from some place where the helo can't land. They can hoist up to 272 kilos of weight."

"Wait a minute. They pick up two people at a time. That 272 pounds isn't gonna hack it with two people."

"No, it's 272 kilos, not 272 pounds, and there's 2.2 pounds to a kilogram. That 272 kilos is 598 pounds."

"How long is the line?"

"Sixty-one meters."

"You've heard about it. Now you are going to do it."

They had three teams of men and two teams of women ready for the op. They knew the terminology, they knew the aircraft, they practiced using the hoist to get into the helos. They could scramble into their seats in the helos rapidly, day or night. All they needed now was to learn where Borst was.

At this point, Kristen and Kaamisha changed clothing from their Army BDU's, Battle Dress Uniforms, into traditional Afghani garb, including the underwear and shoes. The burqas weren't new. They carried local Afghani currency. They had no dollars and no euros. They carried no other currency in their person or in their bags other than Afghani. They carried no American or European soaps, perfumes, or toiletries. Their hairbrushes and combs were bought locally. They brought no English language books or papers. Concealed in the lining of their luggage was one map with GPS grid points of the areas around Kandahar.

Before the women moved to Kandahar, the CIA provided intel that Borst had moved into high terrain north of Bagram Air Base. They deployed two teams of men into the suspected area. It was bad intel and the op turned into a nightmare quickly. The Taliban had them nearly surrounded and their only escape was to go up a rock face and then climb a chimney higher up. Their speed and their training enabled their escape. They managed to get a call for help on the radios and the Black Hawk crew picked them up.

They got back to Bagram Air Base and debriefed the mission with the Sergeant Major. It was about then that Sergeant Rogers came in with an intel message saying that they had mistakenly been following a person who looked like Borst, likely his brother. That meant the need for good intel was as urgent as ever.

Kandahar, Afghanistan

The two teams of women left Bagram Air Base before dawn the next day, in dusty, old vehicles. They drove southwest for approximately 350 miles to arrive in Kandahar. The agency provided a different house for each team of women. Kandahar is the second most populous city in Afghanistan, with a population of over 600,000. The plan was to keep the teams well separated and to allow them to operate independently. That way if one of the teams were compromised, it wouldn't affect the other.

Both teams had the same objective and the same procedure. They would shop for food and necessities in the local markets. They would make several purchases in places that were well separated from each other. When they purchased a lot more food than they could use, they would pass off the extra to the poor.

Kristen was uncomfortable in the burqa, but it concealed her body and her face well. People would not suspect that she was an American soldier. Kaamisha did the shopping. She became comfortable buying food and occasionally an article like a scarf of a purse. She was speaking Dari, her native language, and it allowed her to blend in.

Kristen had been the leader when she and Kaamisha were back in the States, running, hiking, and shooting. In Kandahar, Kaamisha took the lead.

"Kristen, stop talking in English! When we are in the streets, just be quiet. I'll do the talking. You won't draw attention to yourself by being silent. It's normal for us women to have someone travel with us in the streets. We don't go out alone. You can keep your face covered and no one will know who you are."

The women walked from their house to the local markets a few times a day. They kept their ears open for anything that would tell them where Borst was. Every afternoon they gave some of the extra food to the poor women they saw on the streets. It wasn't in the markets that they got their first tip. It was from a homeless lady.

"Thank you," the old woman said. "You and that nice soldier are the only ones who give me anything."

"Soldier?"

"Yes, you can tell. I think he works for the big leader," the old woman said.

The agency put surveillance on the old woman. They were rewarded with a sighting of a man who was giving food to the poor during Ramadan. They watched his vehicle from a satellite and noticed where it was parked. They found a vehicle that was the same make and model as the one they tracked. They trained Stinko how to put a tracker on that type of vehicle. When night fell, Abdul and two other men wore night vision goggles and provided backup. Stinko crawled in the dirt, in the dead of night, and placed a tracker on the man's vehicle. The man had apparently come to town to pick up supplies. The Agency followed the tracker to Borst's village. At the time they weren't sure it was Borst's, but they were willing to check it out.

Chapter 12

"I HATE GETTING SHOT AT!" Abdul shouted."

The bullet from the Taliban rifle hit the rock near Abdul's face and opened up a cut that started bleeding on his forehead.

"Up! Up!" Stinko shouted.

"I know!" Abdul shouted back.

It wasn't like they had a choice. Going left, right, or down would have run them right into the enemy.

The attack plan went to hell before it even got started. Gomez and Gojar, the backup guys from the GG Team, were discovered by a boy who was watching goats. The boy got word to his father's friend, who got word to Borst, who rousted out every man in the village. With rifles. It got ugly fast. The Americans were nearly surrounded before they even knew they had been discovered.

The attack was planned for shortly after sunrise, when the light would favor good vision for a sniper shot. Borst was still operating not far from Kandahar, in the southern part of the Hindu Kush. The elevations were not extreme. The backup team was supposed to locate Borst, and Stinko and Abdul were supposed to move into position unseen, make the shot, and escape to the helo.

The problem with this plan was that it was in terrain that provided very little cover. After Gomez and Gojar were seen above the village, Borst positioned his best shooters in known firing positions, and they opened up on the Americans before they could get set up for a shot.

This was the second time that Abdul and Stinko had to make a rapid escape when the plan went sideways. They climbed at a rate that their enemy couldn't match and provided covering fire for Gomez and Gojar as the slower team tried to catch up. The other team was too slow. They were shot during their attempt to escape. Stinko and Abdul were able to climb up a rock face then circle around the mountain and get picked up by the Black Hawk aircrew. They were taken to a site near Kandahar, then picked up by a car to be taken into the city.

Borst got a report as his shooters returned to the village. "Well?"

"We got two of them. Two got away."

"Got away? How?"

"They climbed the wall."

"The wall? Nobody can climb the wall."

"They did. Fast. After that they were gone."

"What about the two that you got? Americans?"

"One of them looked like an American. The other looks like a local guy."

"Well, you know how to get around the wall. You did that, right?"

"Yes, but they were gone."

"They must know our terrain. Maybe that's why they travel so fast."

"They were fast. I've never seen anybody go that fast."

Borst was silent for a moment.

"We have to move. Now that they know where we are, they can bomb the place or shoot it from their helicopters."

The American group met in a safe house in Kandahar. The Sergeant Major was grim.

"We knew that Gomez and Gujar were hit because we saw that on a satellite feed. We didn't know how bad it was until we saw them buried."

"We know where they're buried, right? Can their bodies be returned to the States for burial?" Kristen asked.

"Yeah, that's the plan, but first we got to finish this op."

The group consisted of Stinko, Abdul, Kristen, Kaamisha, the Sergeant Major, Sergeant Rogers, and a representative from the Agency.

"What's the plan now?"

"We go back to buying food again. We start surveillance on the woman who got food from the soldier. We are almost back to square one."

"Not exactly, Sergeant Rogers said. We have the tracker on the guy's car. Why not watch where it parks at night, and put a couple more trackers on the nearby vehicles, so we have a better chance of finding where they are?"

"The agency rep nodded his head. "Yes, we can keep track of several vehicles."

The plan may have been a good one, but it was never initiated. The vehicle with the tracker moved that same day, and drove toward the northeast for hours, to the high country of the Hindu Kush.

At a meeting the next morning the Sergeant Major informed them that they were moving back to Bagram Air Base.

"Borst has been known to use the high country north of Bagram when we get close to him. We believe that he has relatives in the area. He makes more money from drugs down south here, but the high and lonely is where his kinfolk are. So, this move is consistent with what we have seen him do before."

The Sergeant Major explained what they could be dealing with: "Many peaks in the area are between 14,500 and 17,000 feet (5200m). Near Kabul, in the west, they are slightly lower. In the east they get up to 19,700 feet (6000m). Bagram Air Base is about 36 miles north of Kabul, much closer to the anticipated op area."

"We are going to move up to Bagram, get moved in, have some American food if you wish, and then move the ladies into the towns in the Hindu Kush and buy some food."

"Uh, I wouldn't do that," Rogers interjected."

"Do what Rogers?"

"Eat American food. If you eat American food, you smell like a westerner. Your hands, your clothes, your poop, all western. It compromises your safety."

"I can handle the local food, Kristen said."

"Yeah, same here, Stinko said."

Abdul and Kaamisha nodded.

"All right. We'll see that you get the local stuff. Pack up. I can get you a ride to a place where we can pick you up by helo and fly you up to Bagram."

"One more thing, while I have the group together. Is there any possibility we could get this guy alive?"

"If we did, we would have to make him unconscious with some sort of a sedative, then carry him," Stinko volunteered. "The exfil would be much slower."

"What's the point?" Rogers asked.

"Could we turn him? Get him to work with us for peace?"

"Abdul? Thoughts?"

"The Taliban are tribal. They likely would not follow a leader of another tribe. And I don't want to give him a chance to live to spread his poison. Borst stole the crops and the money from many farmers in Afghanistan. He stole the crop from Wasim, my fiancée's father. They took the money that he got from his crop another time. They hit him and broke his nose. Borst's men tried to rape my fiancée. They beat her sister. They injured her mother."

"OK. So, saving the guy probably wouldn't gain us a darn thing," the Sergeant Major concluded.

They looked at a map before they left the room. They noticed that the Dorah Pass between Pakistan and Afghanistan was at 14,000 feet. The Hindu Kush was the area where the Taliban and Al Qaeda grew. It was a scene of warfare in modern times. In ancient times the area was Buddhist. It is now predominantly Muslim. In 2001 the Taliban Islamists destroyed the giant rock carvings of Buddha in the southern and western ends of the Hindu Kush.

The area they would operate in was home to a million tribesmen who traditionally paid no taxes and owed allegiance to nobody. In the late 1980's they changed loyalty to the Taliban and Al Qaeda, which transformed the region in Afghanistan and West Pakistan to a jihadist state. The locals acknowledged Mullah Omar of the Taliban and Osama bin Laden of Al Qaeda as their spiritual and political emirs.

The Black Hawk pilot "Blackie" and his crew gave the operators a ride back to Bagram Air Base. Stinko and Abdul were sharing a room in a trailer. On the wall was a map of the air base and another of the entire area.

Abdul was standing in front of the map of the Bagram Air Base. "Stinko, you see this?"

Stinko joined him in front of the map. Abdul pointed at the field elevation, 4895 feet (1490m).

Abdul looked at him.

"Yeah, I got it. I'll talk to the Sergeant Major."

With the approval of the Sergeant Major, they arranged for a helo flight up to an elevation of 10,000 feet. They brought with them a tent, sleeping bags, sleeping pads, ponchos, a three-day supply of fruits and vegetables, nuts, local meats, beans, several pairs of socks, enough jerry cans with water to float a boat, cook stoves with propane, their rifles, lots of spare ammo, radios, cell phones, and Stinko's chin-up bar.

Stinko gave Abdul his assessment of the situation: "They won't have good intel on Borst for a couple of days. We can do some good workouts for a while."

They hiked from the 10,000 foot level up to the 14,000 foot level, had lunch, shot several rounds for target practice, and hiked back to their camp at 10,000 feet in the late afternoon. They repeated the exercise the next day.

"We are doing the same thing the Himalayan mountaineers do aren't we?" Abdul asked.

"Yeah. Hike high, sleep low. That's what they do. Although, their base camp is at 14,000 feet because they have to hike up to 29,000 feet. We don't have to go that high. I saw a movie that showed the first team that summited Everest. The first two were Tenzing Norgay and Edmund Hilary. Tenzing Norgay was smoking a cigarette at 24,000 feet."

"So, you got a cigarette?" Abdul asked.

"You want one?"

"Sure, it worked for Tenzing Norgay. It should work for me!"

Stinko found a place to set up his chin-up bar. He emptied out his pack, put 25 pounds of rocks in it, and did three sets of pull-ups to exhaustion.

"When I was at college, they didn't serve any food on Sunday night, so we had to go to a restaurant to buy food. I used to challenge guys in my dorm to a pull-up contest.

If they win, I would buy the Sunday night dinner. If I win, they would buy."

"Did you lose?"

No.

"How did you do it?"

"I would make the other guy go first. He would do 10 pull-ups. I would struggle to barely get to do 11, but I would win. After I beat everyone on the floor of my dorm, I would challenge the guys who lived on other floors. This worked for the whole year that I was there."

"How many pull-ups can you do?" Abdul asked.

"Forty-four."

Stinko and Abdul both had radios and cell phones. They checked in three times a day.

———◆———

Now a soldier's spirit is keenest in the morning, by noonday it has begun to flag, and in the evening his mind is bent on only returning to camp.

When a fire breaks out inside the enemy's camp, respond at once with an attack from without."

Sun Tzu
The Art of War

The Sergeant Major recalled Stinko and Abdul from their high-altitude camp. This time it was the pilot with the callsign "Thumper" in his Pave Hawk helicopter who picked them up.

The Sergeant Major started the meeting. Everyone was in attendance, including the air crews, plus Kristen and Kaamisha, who replaced the team that was killed.

"We lost a signal on the vehicle when it got about 168 miles north of Kabul, in the Hindu Kush. It drove to a small village called Korogah. That can be spelled about six different ways. The town has all of 140 people. Its time zone is plus 4:30, like all of Afghanistan. It's elevated, and the terrain around it is higher yet."

"We lost the signal, but the signal came back on the third day. We assumed that they had parked it under a house or under a building that blocked the emitter. We made a comparison of the vehicles in town before and after the time that this vehicle arrived. There are five more vehicles that we can see that are in town now, versus what was there a week ago. So, it isn't the greatest intel in the world, but we want to check it out."

"Our plan is to get into the house where this car gets parked and see if our bad guy or his soldiers are there."

"Why don't you fly one of those robot insects in there and check it out?"

"Last time we did that they found the darn thing and smashed it. We think a dawn raid would be better."

"Abdul, you want to tell them what you told me?" Stinko asked.

"Dawn OK. Evening better."

"Why?"

"Number one: In evening, men tired. Fajr to Maghrib, 15 hours. That's morning prayer to evening prayer. It's Ramadan. They are fasting. No food. Men tired."

The Sergeant Major had spent enough time in Afghanistan, and spoke enough Dari, to explain to his people that Fajr and Maghrib are first prayer and fourth prayer.

"Number two. We run into house. We see one team of Taliban. Only one team. Not good. But, if we start a fire, or maybe make an explosion, like a bomb. Everyone hear it. Men run out of houses. We see all teams."

Nobody spoke for a while. Stinko said, "I like Abdul's plan."

The Sergeant Major looked at the air crews. He said, "I want to hear from the air crews. Let's start with the junior guys first. If the senior guys say something, the junior guys always shut up. So, let's start with the the PJ's, the pararescue men. You got a problem with picking people up at dusk?"

"No. Not at all."

"Can you pick people up after dark?"

"Sure."

"Pilots you OK with a dusk pickup?"

"Sure."

"Night?"

"Much more dangerous due to terrain, but if we agree on an exfil point ahead of time we can scope it out before it's dark."

"How about this? Stinko spoke up. We blow something up at about sundown. They come out. We shoot from a range that is acceptable to Abdul but would be beyond their accurate range. We get their attention, and then start climbing. They follow us, like they did before. That's when Thumper and his merry men in their Pave Hawk helo come around the mountain and give them an example of air to ground gunnery."

Kristen added her idea: "If Kaamisha and I are in the right place when you set off the explosion, we can use binoculars or run a camera to see if Borst comes out of the house and starts pursuing you."

"If the helo doesn't get there soon enough, you could be caught between the Taliban and the village."

"I'm a soldier, drawing soldier's pay" was Kristen's response.

"Any reason we couldn't do this tomorrow night?"

"There's no reason we can't do it tonight," was Kristen's remark.

"Do we need a go ahead nod from the three star?" Blackie, the Black Hawk pilot asked.

The Sergeant Major answered. "We are going to tell them what we will do. We won't ask them."

The Black Hawk pilot wasn't convinced. For him, RHIP (rank has its privileges), which includes writing the plan.

The Sergeant Major put to rest the pilot's unease. "It's been our experience that if we ask the brass to come up with a plan, they do. However, the plans are better when the guys whose boots are on the ground make up the plan. What I will do is send them a message after the op is already in progress, saying, UNODIR (Unless Otherwise Directed) we will initiate our operation tonight."

Northern Hindu Kush, Afghanistan

The town was about 130 miles from Bagram Air Base. Since the Black Hawk cruised at 174 mph, with a range of 360 miles, it was doable range from a pilot's perspective. Both the Black Hawk and the Pave Hawk can do in-flight refueling. The pilots arranged for them to fly up to a place that was fairly close to the town but not within earshot of it, then do in-flight refueling from a C-130 tanker aircraft out of Bagram.

Stinko, Abdul, and the KK Team inserted into the area together from Blackie's helicopter. The helicopter used the high terrain of the area to hide behind during the transit to the op area. After dropping off the operators, the two helos did their refueling and set down in an area five miles from the town, behind the mountain, out of sight and out of earshot from the town. They shut down their engines, got out of the chopper, and relaxed. The real action wouldn't start until dusk. They had hours to kill. The crew of the AC-130 gunship was sitting in the aircraft in a ready alert status at the end of the runway at Bagram Air Base.

The four operators were on the ground before noon, but it took them the whole afternoon to creep into a position where they could see the village. They made a great effort to stay out of sight. Sniper work frequently requires hours of setup before a shot. This was no different.

"Abdul," Stinko whispered. "Figure out where you want to be for the shot. I'll figure out the exit route from there."

After Abdul picked his spot, Stinko crawled back to where the women were. He selected his preferred escape route, then picked a spot where Kristen and Kaamisha would be able to ambush the Taliban if they pursued Stinko and Abdul.

The village had a large tank for gasoline, which made a lovely target since it was elevated to use gravity to get gasoline into the car or truck and eliminate the need for a pump. Stinko and Abdul got into good firing positions. Based on a prearranged signal, Stinko clicked his radio once. Kristen clicked once in response. Ready.

Stinko spoke briefly into his radio.

"Execute in one mike." It was H-hour. Sundown in the Hindu Kush.

There was one click on the radio from Thumper in the Pave Hawk, and one click from Blackie in the Black Hawk. "Ready."

Abdul looked at Stinko and nodded. "Ready."

The plan was for all four operators to fire simultaneously.

Stinko spoke into his radio, "Three, two, one, fire!"

The 5.56mm round fired by the M4 carbine travels at 2970 feet per second. It didn't lose much velocity traveling downhill in the thin air. It covered the 800 feet in roughly a quarter of a second. The vapor in the tank exploded violently, causing the entire tank to burst into flame. Within a minute men emerged from the houses, carrying rifles. Anyone with a rifle was a target. The operators started picking off anyone with a rifle who did not take cover.

The Taliban obviously had foreseen such a contingency. They used the cover that the houses and rocks provided to start pursuit of the shooters. Within a minute the numbers favored the Taliban. They were able to get 20 people in pursuit. Abdul and Stinko took out four of them before moving to higher terrain. Sixteen to go. Stinko and Abdul crawled into another preselected firing position. They opened fire from there, which drew the Taliban forward, and directly into Kristen's field of fire. Kaamisha and Kristen used their weapons with deadly effect. Twelve to go.

"THUMPER WE NEED YOU!" Stinko screamed on the radio.

"With you in one mike!" Thumper replied. They went airborne when they heard the explosion and were already enroute.

Stinko clarified the situation using his radio, "We are going uphill. Guys below us are bad guys." It was the planned words they had agreed on for this stage of the operation.

"Roger that Stinko!" Thumper replied.

"I see you Thumper. Kristen, are you ready?" Stinko asked on the radio.

"Roger. Ready!" Kristen replied.

Stinko counted down. "OK. Three, two one, WE GO NOW!"

Stinko and Abdul scrambled uphill as fast as they could go. The Taliban started pursuit, and realized they couldn't match the speed of their enemy. The endless workouts at high elevation paid off.

The Taliban followed, and now realized that a helicopter had them sighted. They took cover. It didn't matter to the Pave Hawk crew. Their 4000 rounds per minute from the air obliterated the enemy.

"Cease fire! Cease fire!" Stinko shouted on the radio. "Did anyone see Borst? Abdul?"

"Negative."

"Kaamisha? Did you see Borst?" Kaamisha had binoculars.

"Negative."

Stinko gave direction based on experience: "Don't get too close to the bodies over there. Let's check them out from a distance."

Nobody could identify Borst among the bodies on the ground.

"There might have been a guy who came out of a house and went back in," Kaamisha said. "Everything happened fast."

"Thumper, what's your time to bingo?"

"About an hour and forty-five. I can in-flight refuel before RTB (return to base)."

"Roger. We are going to check out the village."

The sun was down but there was adequate light to make out details like doors, windows, cars, and porch railings.

"Kaamisha, which house had the guy who went back in?"

"That one," she said and pointed.

Their training had been in mountain warfare, not urban warfare. They realized this was going to be dangerous.

The house had three rooms. Stinko and Abdul burst into the main room, one going left, one right. "Clear!" They entered the room to the right, pushed open the door and paused a moment. Then they burst through the door. One went left, one right. "Clear!"

Kristen and Kaamisha entered the room on the left. Kristen got blasted in the chest from a woman holding an AK47. Kristen fell to the floor. Kaamisha put three rounds into the woman's chest, then three more into her head after she fell. Stinko and Abdul entered the room.

There was a wood armoire on the side of the room. Stinko nodded to Abdul, who raised his rifle into a firing position. Stinko counted on his fingers three, two, one, and yanked the closet door open.

Borst stood inside the closet with his rifle pointed up. Borst pulled his rifle down to shoot. Abdul shot him right between the eyes.

"Abdul, is it Borst?" Stinko asked, although he already knew the answer.

"Yes."

They ran over to Kristen, who was on the floor. Kristen?

"Jesus that hurts," Kristen moaned.

"Are you OK?"

"Uh, yeah. I think so."

"Kaamisha, Abdul, get to the door. See if anyone else is coming!" Stinko directed.

Stinko kneeled down by Kristen.

"Kristen, get your hand under your shirt. Are you bleeding?

"Stinko, loosen the flak jacket," Kristen asked. Her voice was weak.

The Kevlar vest stopped the bullet, as it should. The AK47 round that hit her wasn't the armor piercing variety.

"Kristen, check. Are you bleeding?"

Her hand went under her shirt and came out. Clean.

Let me see your shirt.

"Stinko, you just want to get your hand under my shirt."

"Not a bad idea."

That got a smile from Kristen.

"Let's get back into the game," Kristen said. "Help me get this Kevlar vest on again."

The local inhabitants stayed in their houses and didn't open windows or doors. One kid got inquisitive and opened his front door. A burst of gunfire from the Pave Hawk that hit the ground in front of the door convinced him to close the door and leave it shut. There were no other curious people after that.

"Kristen, Kaamisha, cover us!" Stinko instructed. "There is a spot down the road where the helos can land. Abdul and I will collect all the weapons. We will put as many weapons as we can into one car, drive it down the road, and unload all of it into the helos. We need to find some car keys first."

"Keys! There! On the wall!" Kaamisha pointed to the hooks on the wall with keys.

"Let me take some pictures of Borst first," Kristen said. "Then I'll cover you."

"Kaamisha, get some hair and skin for DNA samples," Kristen said.

The exfil went smoothly. The helos had enough fuel to make it to Bagram with plenty to spare.

They debriefed in the trailer at Bagram. They covered everything. They discussed what went right, what went wrong, what they needed to change. Rogers recorded the debrief on video. He also jotted down a few notes in case the video didn't work.

The Sergeant Major looked at Kaamisha and said, "You really blasted the lady with the rifle?"

"Blasted the hell out of her," Stinko said.

"Her M4 was set for three round bursts," Abdul said. "Normally automatic fire climbs up and to the right. Her shots didn't even climb. Good job of holding down on the target, Kaamisha," Abdul said.

The Sergeant Major had been waiting to say this: "You did a terrific job. You all did. I knew you would. In fact, we have another job we want you to get into right away."

Stinko replied, "We have something to do first, Sergeant Major. Abdul and I have a couple of women in the States who need to get married. We are going to need you to be there."

Printed in the United States
by Baker & Taylor Publisher Services